PETER RABBIT™

BASED ON THE

MAJOR NEW MOVIE

PUFFIN

PETER RABBIT™

BASED ON THE
MAJOR NEW MOVIE

PUFFIN BOOKS

UK | USA | Canada | Ireland | Australia
India | New Zealand | South Africa

Puffin Books is part of the Penguin Random House group of companies
whose addresses can be found at global.penguinrandomhouse.com.

www.penguin.co.uk www.puffin.co.uk www.ladybird.co.uk

First published 2018
003

With thanks to Fiona Phillipson

Printed in Great Britain by Clays Ltd, St Ives plc

A CIP catalogue record for this book is available from the British Library

ISBN: 978–0–241–33072–2

All correspondence to:
Puffin Books
Penguin Random House Children's
80 Strand, London WC2R 0RL

CONTENTS

Chapter One

RABBITS RULE

It's a beautiful day in the most perfect corner of the English countryside. The sun is shining over the rolling hills, emerald-green fields and rivers of the Lake District. The sweet birdsong of a flock of sparrows can be heard as they fly in formation over this special part of England.

All is peaceful until a furry ball of fluff tears through the field. That furry ball of fluff is our hero, Peter Rabbit. He is a young rabbit in a blue coat and no trousers. A rabbit who is clearly on a mission as he races through the green countryside of his home. He's determined and clever as he outfoxes Mr. Tod, a fox who is hungry for rabbit, bounds up a tree past Squirrel Nutkin and scampers towards a stream, thinking nothing of stepping on Jemima Puddle-duck to reach the other side.

A frog sits calmly on a lily pad, fishing in the stream.

'Garden, eh?' says Jeremy Fisher to Peter. 'He's gonna get you one of these days.'

'Nothing scares me,' laughs Peter, before jumping in fright as a fish leaps clear of the water. Well, nothing on *dry* land scares our hero.

Peter bounds on to a stone wall only to find his mission briefy halted by Mrs. Tiggy-winkle, a hedgehog in a white apron. But you will soon learn that our hero is never stopped for long.

Peter races through the lush green fields and speeds up to a tree where he finds his cousin, Benjamin. This is a special tree because it has the best view of Peter's target. Peter looks down and sees an old man hunched over a lawnmower. The old man has skin that has been wrinkled by the sun and wears a giant frown. His name is Old Mr. McGregor and his vegetable garden is the target of Peter's mission.

'I don't think you're going to have enough time,' says Benjamin, a worried look on his face. 'I really think you should call this one off. Wait till next time.'

'You worry too much,' says Peter.

'One of us has to,' says Benjamin, but Peter has already run off. Benjamin jumps after him, but ends up falling out of the tree. Benjamin is a wise and supportive bunny, with ears that look like they have been put on backwards!

Benjamin is not the only member of Peter's family out today. Just near Old Mr. McGregor's garden there are three bunnies trying to reach one very pathetic-looking blackberry at the top of a tall bush. Each bunny is standing on another bunny. This means it will probably end with someone falling over.

'Higher,' says the first bunny, Cotton-tail.

'Why am I always at the bottom?' lisps the third bunny, Flopsy.

'Because you're the youngest,' says the second bunny, Mopsy.

'By sixteen seconds!' argues Flopsy.

Peter runs up to his three sisters just as Flopsy falls to the ground. She brings Mopsy and Cotton-tail down with her. The three bunnies shake off the fall and look at their big brother. They all love Peter Rabbit.

'I'm going in,' says Peter.

'We found some blackberries,' says Flopsy, holding up two dried-up, wrinkled berries that do not look very tasty at all.

'Those aren't blackberries. Those are the ghosts of blackberries,' says Peter. He knows he can find better food for his sisters. 'That,' he says, looking down at Mr. McGregor's vegetable garden. 'That is what we deserve. And that is what we shall have.'

'Can I come in with you this time?' asks Cotton-tail.

'No. I need you as lookouts, like always. I don't want to put you in danger when I look death in the face for the good of the family. Now, get into positions. It's gonna be a fun one!' says Peter, winking at them all.

He is excited about his mission, but he knows he must keep his family safe. He has to go into Mr. McGregor's garden by himself.

Later, the three sisters take up their positions as Peter's lookouts. They have done it many times before and know exactly where to stand. They watch as their brother approaches the gate to Mr. McGregor's garden.

Peter looks towards the mower and sees that Mr. McGregor still has more grass to cut. He crawls under the gate and makes it into the garden. With all the energy he has, Peter starts tossing vegetables over the fence and into Benjamin's waiting arms. Benjamin catches them like an expert and throws them to the triplets in the trees.

'OK, that's enough now,' Benjamin says as more and more vegetables fly over from the garden. 'Why don't you come back?' But Peter just keeps throwing them. 'We're not even that hungry! This is entirely too much food!'

Meanwhile, Mr. McGregor continues to mow the grass. He has no idea that our hero is stealing all his vegetables! Peter spots the rabbit traps that Mr. McGregor has scattered around his garden. He happily dances over them. There isn't a trap in the world that can stop Peter!

But then the mower stops. The garden becomes silent. Peter and the other rabbits look at Mr. McGregor. They watch as the mean old farmer checks beneath his mower and curses to himself. Mr. McGregor leaves the mower and walks into the vegetable garden through the gate. He is walking right towards Peter Rabbit. Peter is a sitting duck. Or, rather, rabbit.

The triplets let out a gasp. They need to help their brother! Flopsy and Mopsy use their arms – and ears – to send helpful signals to Peter. As the old man moves right, the sisters signal left. Peter follows, until . . . SNAP! He accidentally sets off a trap. Old Mr. McGregor turns around. He knows something is wrong. He knows something, or someone, is in his garden.

'Rah-bbit!' yells Old Mr. McGregor. Peter searches for his lookouts and sees his sisters and Benjamin all have their ears pinned back. This is the sign of danger. Peter's in trouble now.

SNAP! Another trap is set off. But this time it is not by Peter. Instead, Cotton-tail has set the trap off by throwing a radish into it from the fence.

The noise is a distraction, and it works! Mr. McGregor turns towards the sound. A few more diversions from Cotton-tail and Peter is almost at the gate. But then his mischievousness gets the better of him, just like it always does.

Peter spots a ripe, juicy tomato. He just has to have it. Peter lunges for the tomato. The other rabbits signal for him to NOT DO THAT! But he is Peter Rabbit. And he does exactly that.

Benjamin tries to cover his eyes with his floppy ears.

'I can't look!' he says.

Old Mr. McGregor is now blocking Peter's path to the gate. His sisters signal to him as he tries to avoid the farmer. Mr. McGregor is almost upon him. Peter is going to be caught!

SNAP! Cotton-tail has tossed one more radish, triggering a trap in the other direction. Peter's path is clear once again. Mr. McGregor's beard is touching the ground as he peers at the trap. Peter can't help himself. He carefully places one of the traps underneath Mr. McGregor's beard and taps it with a nearby carrot. SNAP!

Mr. McGregor yelps out in pain and spins around. His beard is clamped tightly in the trap.

'Rah-bbit! I'm going to put you in a pie!' he yells, struggling to free his beard. Peter scampers off as fast as he can towards the gate. But he still can't help himself and glances back to enjoy seeing Mr. McGregor with his beard in the trap . . . and gets himself tangled in a gooseberry net.

Old Mr. McGregor is furious. He uses all his strength to swing his rake right at Peter Rabbit. Cotton-tail tries more diversions but they don't help. The rake pins Peter by his jacket to the ground.

Is this the end for Peter Rabbit? Of course not. Peter manages to slide out of his jacket and, leaving it behind, races under the gate. He's free! Just as the rabbits are thinking the worst is over, the gate bursts open. Old Mr. McGregor, holding his rake, hurls it down again towards Peter Rabbit. Only this time, Peter swoops up from the ground, narrowly avoiding death. It's like he's flying! Like he has super powers! But rabbits do not have super powers.

What they do have is guardian angels. And this particular guardian angel is human and has swept Peter Rabbit up into the air. This is Bea.

'Oh, it's you,' says Mr. McGregor.

'Morning, Mr. McGregor! Beautiful day!' says the lovely but tough Bea.

Bea is Mr. McGregor's next-door neighbour and they couldn't be more different.

'Give me that rabbit,' snarls Mr. McGregor.

Bea is holding Peter tightly. She looks at him with love and concern.

'Are you OK?' Bea asks Peter. She isn't scared of Old Mr. McGregor. Peter's eyes tell her that he is 'totally fine'. They also say 'thank you'.

'This is my garden,' shouts Mr. McGregor.

'Let me pass that along,' says Bea. She turns to look at Peter. 'This is *his* garden.' She turns her attention once more to Old Mr. McGregor. 'There. I think we're all on the same page and these rabbits will now surrender their natural instinct to feed themselves,' she says, sarcastically.

'Next time will be the last time,' warns Mr. McGregor. He bends down to pick up all the vegetables Peter had thrown over to Benjamin.

'Nice melons,' says Bea.

Mr. McGregor turns back and hits at a huge melon with his rake in frustration. It explodes everywhere. Shards of melon cover the rabbits. They recoil until they have a taste. The melon is delicious! They start licking everything they can off their faces. Mr. McGregor returns to his garden with a huff and slams the gate shut.

'Always great talking to you!' Bea calls after him. Her last words are drowned out by a loud clap of thunder. Rain clouds fill the sky and a downpour begins.

'Come on, sweeties. I'll get you something to drink,' says Bea, hurrying everyone towards her cottage and out of the rain.

Chapter Two
DANGER IN THE GARDEN

Inside her cottage, Bea uses her fluffiest towels to dry off the rabbits.

'You can't keep going in there. That was almost it for you this time,' says a concerned Bea to the rabbits. She pours blackberry spa water into a bowl that is used especially for these occasions. Four glorious blackberries plop out. Each bunny lunges for their berry. Mopsy and Flopsy fight over one of the biggest ones.

Bea looks at the bunnies, her eyes filled with love. She may live alone but she isn't lonely. Not with her favourite furry animals always around.

The cottage is filled with Bea's half-finished portraits. Bea is an artist. She moved to the country to work on her paintings but her talent does not seem to lie in portraits. There are many other finished paintings in her cottage. They are mostly of animals in clothes. And then, mostly of rabbits. Some even look familiar.

Peter looks at one painting in particular. It is a portrait of a rabbit family. Peter's family, from long ago. A time that Peter can remember as if it was yesterday. The whole family together, his mum and dad, with his little sisters, Flopsy, Mopsy, and Cotton-tail . . . and himself, Peter. They would all frolic next to Mr. McGregor's manor. The rabbits were happy, laughing and playing. Peter's father would teach them to walk on two legs, and Peter's mother would mark how tall they grew with their paw prints on the wall of their burrow.

Peter and his father would gather juicy plums from the tree behind Mr. McGregor's manor, filling a basket to take home to the family. But one day, the tree shook and shook and a tractor began to plough over the field where the rabbits had once frolicked. Not only that, the mean old man then built a fence around the plum tree!

Peter recalls the night he had watched through the window of the burrow as his dad had sneaked under the fence and into Mr. McGregor's garden. Then, Mr. McGregor had appeared, looming over Peter's father with a rake in his hand. Peter now remembers seeing that rake come down with a terrible clang.

Peter had run to the McGregor manor and looked

through the window only to see Mrs. McGregor serving Mr. McGregor rabbit pie.

Peter's eyes had filled with tears as he had noticed his dad's blue jacket lying on the ground of the garden. Peter had picked it up and put it on. It was too big, but Peter wore it anyway.

Peter shakes his head, trying to get the terrible memories out of his mind. He is soon back in Bea's cottage. Safe. He looks down at where his jacket should have been. His dad's jacket lost in Old Mr. McGregor's garden forever.

Peter looks up again at a different painting. This time a portrait of his mother and father. Bea comes over and kneels down beside Peter.

'I promise I'll always be there for you,' she says softly as she strokes Peter's head.

Bea is gentle and very protective of her rabbits. Almost like a mother. In fact, Bea has been a mum to them ever since their own mother died. Bea looks out of her cottage window. The rain has finally stopped and the sun is shining through the clouds.

'Ooh, the sun's out,' says Bea. The rabbits cheer up. The gloom is lifted from the day.

Later that day, Bea and her beloved rabbits go for a bike ride through the countryside. They frolic next to the bike's wheels, hop on to walls as she rides past and even race Bea before Peter jumps into her basket.

'Isn't it beautiful today?' she says. Peter nods. 'I swear sometimes you can understand me.'

The rabbits *can* understand her but they don't let on. It's the only way animals and humans can get along. If we all knew what we were saying about each other, it would be chaos. Just ask the dinosaurs!

Back in the burrow, each bunny hangs their jacket on a hook on the wall. All except Peter. They look at him with sad eyes.

'Sorry, Peter. I'll make you a new one,' offers Mopsy.

'If you'd let me go into the garden with you, it never would have happened. Why don't you ever let me go in with you?' demands Cotton-tail, just like she always does.

'You remember what happened to Dad, right?' says Peter.

'But *you* go in all the time,' says Cotton-tail, crossing her paws.

But Peter won't change his mind, just like the big, over-protective brother he is.

'Anyway, it's just a jacket. Dad's still here.'

Peter puts his hand on his heart.

The burrow becomes very quiet for a moment.

'Now, who wants to play ball in the house?' says Peter, tossing a ball towards his sisters. It's nice to have fun after their terrible, and frightening, encounter with Mr. McGregor. The lack of parental supervision that comes from your parents being put in a pie has certain advantages.

They play happily for a while, but, as is always the way with these things, someone ends up getting hurt. And this time it's Flopsy who gets a bump on the head, thanks to Mopsy.

Mopsy leans her forehead against Flopsy's and they stay like that for a moment. It's the rabbit way of apologizing. Peter nods to Cotton-tail, who races from the burrow to find something for Flopsy's sore head.

Outside, Cotton-tail runs up to Jeremy Fisher who is sitting on his cold lily pad. It's exactly what she needs. With one quick tug she yanks it out from under him, just like a magician's tablecloth.

'Hey!' cries Jeremy Fisher as he splashes into the water.

'Sorry! Medical emergency,' calls Cotton-tail by way of an explanation. She bursts back into the burrow and hands the lily pad to Mopsy who then puts it on Flopsy's bruise.

'How's that?' asks Mopsy, hoping the cool, soft lily pad will do the trick.

'I'm fine. Think I'm just hungry,' says Flopsy. Peter knows he must look after her. He is the big brother, after all. Peter needs to find food for his family.

Peter slips out from the burrow. He heads towards the blackberry bush that had those sad, shrivelled berries the girls abandoned earlier that day. A flash of blue catches his eye. It's his jacket, his dad's jacket! And it's in Old Mr. McGregor's garden. Not only that, Mr. McGregor has turned it into a scarecrow. Peter only needs one second to think about what to do next. He needs to get that jacket back right away!

Peter sprints to the garden. The gate is open. It seems strange that Mr. McGregor would leave the gate open, but Peter does not question it too much. After all, going through the open gate is easier than scrambling underneath it. Peter runs into the garden, grabs his jacket, puts it on and turns to head back out. BANG!

A sieve falls on top of Peter.

'Got ya, rah-bbit! I knew you'd come,' says Mr. McGregor, pleased with the trap he has set.

Mr. McGregor knew Peter would not be able to resist coming through the open gate for his jacket. Mr. McGregor and Peter are face to face. Peter has never been so scared.

'No one to protect you now. I've got a hankering for pie tonight,' growls Mr. McGregor. Peter cannot see any way out. He cannot believe this is the end. Peter and Mr. McGregor continue to stare at each other.

Just when all hope seems lost, the strangest thing happens. Mr. McGregor's eyes go very, very wide. With an almighty thud, he crashes to the ground. Peter's own eyes grow very, very, wide. He looks down at the old man. What has just happened?

Peter stares at Old Mr. McGregor's face. It seems different somehow. Almost like he's . . . dead. Slowly, Peter reaches out under the sieve and gives Mr. McGregor a poke. Yup. Dead. Peter looks all around the garden. He cannot quite believe what has happened. Could our hero, Peter Rabbit, have just had *another* very lucky escape?

Chapter Three

PARTY TIME!

Peter races home to the burrow and charges through the door. In his paws is a net that is bursting with lots of fruit and vegetables from Mr. McGregor's garden.

'Who wants some blackberries?' exclaims Peter. He takes a minute to catch his breath. 'Or, how about something that is much, much better. And is endless.'

Peter spills out his bounty from inside the net. It's more vegetables than they have ever seen!

'You went to Mr. McGregor's garden?' asks Mopsy. She can't quite believe Peter would go back in there so soon after his narrow escape.

'No, I went into *our* garden,' says Peter, proudly.

'Without lookouts? That's the sort of thing that could get someone killed!' says Benjamin, his voice full of worry for his cousin.

'And it did,' says Peter. He enjoys the suspense for a moment before proudly telling everyone that Mr. McGregor is dead.

'Mr. McGregor's dead?' Mopsy asks.

'I got him,' boasts Peter.

'What? What happened?' asks Benjamin, jumping up with excitement.

Peter starts to tell the story of Old Mr. McGregor's death but things get a little muddy in the retelling. As Peter re-enacts a scene that is worthy of a rabbit Oscar, Benjamin, Flopsy, Mopsy and Cotton-tail are captivated. Peter lunges as if he impaled the farmer on his own rake, when in actual fact he can't even claim to have given the old man a fright.

In all probability, Old Mr. McGregor's unhealthy lifestyle for the last seventy-eight years is more to blame for his death than Peter Rabbit. Still, Peter was not about to let facts get in the way of a good story! Either way, the ending is the same. Old Mr. McGregor is dead and the garden is theirs again!

The others all cheer and gobble up the fruit and vegetables that Peter has collected.

'But save some room. This is only the beginning,' he says.

'I made you a new jacket,' says Mopsy, holding a flowery creation.

Peter, trying not to offend, says, 'It's so good! Wow. But, you know, this is Dad's and all . . .'

Later, they hear the sound of an ambulance outside. Peter leads them all out of the burrow. The rabbits watch as the ambulance drives away from Mr. McGregor's manor. The bunnies sneak under the gate and into Mr. McGregor's garden. Their garden. A hush falls as they take it all in.

'Whoa,' they all sigh. They've never been so close to so much food.

'Come on in. It's your garden,' says Peter.

They all take another step, and then race around the garden, enjoying everything and anything they can get their hands on.

Benjamin shakes the plum tree while Flopsy and Mopsy make snow angels from the fallen fruit. Peter bends down a corn stalk for the others to eat and makes it rain lettuces.

Soon, the noise and commotion the rabbits are making in Mr. McGregor's garden can be heard through the woods. Deer, squirrels, Pigling Bland and Mrs. Tiggy-winkle all drop what they are doing and flock with great excitement towards the noise. They know something good must be happening. They all clamour to get into the garden and are about to jump the fence when Peter stops them in their tracks.

'Whoa, hey! You animals can't come in here,' says Peter. He disappears and reappears at the gate. 'Come in over here,' he says, with a giant grin on his face.

Flopsy and Mopsy open the gate and welcome all the guests into their garden. Then an almighty explosion stops everyone in their tracks. The gate is ripped off its hinges and Felix D'Eer, a big deer with huge antlers, enters the garden. The gate is stuck to his antlers.

'Or here is fine, too, I guess,' says Peter, gesturing to the space where the gate had been.

Felix hurls the gate from his antlers. It hits some peppers, slicing them up and into the air, before they land neatly in the mouths of some waiting squirrels.

Then the sparrows fly through singing. Next, Tommy Brock the badger barrels into the garden, knocking the sparrows over.

'Help yourself to anything,' Peter invites him. 'Try the tomatoes. Who am I talking to? You don't need to be told twice to jump on free food, you lazy badger,' continues Peter, acting like the host with the most.

'I'm not lazy. I'm carrying all these tomatoes,' says Tommy Brock, his pride hurt just a little.

Meanwhile, Mr. Tod approaches.

'Look at you, big fella. Wait, didn't you try to eat me?' Peter asks, his brow wrinkling into a frown. 'Show me your teeth. It *was* you! I knew it. How are you? Let's set aside the food chain for tonight and just come together as one, huh?'

Peter continues to rabbit on. He is hoping to distract Mr. Tod from wanting to take a bite out of him. Peter tosses Mr. Tod a turnip and the fox slinks away just as Pigling Bland waltzes in.

'I see you got your land back. All hail the prodigal son,' says Pigling Bland, a rather skinny pig dressed as quite the dandy in a purple velvet jacket.

'No big deal,' says Peter.

'A very big deal. You killed Mr. McGregor,' says Pigling Bland.

'Well, he was alive when I went in the garden, dead when I left. You join the dots,' says Peter casually.

'The compost heap is right over there, pig. Got your name on it,' says Benjamin.

'Oh no, I couldn't possibly. I'm working on this celery stalk,' says Pigling Bland, desperately trying to not be a pig, even though that is exactly what he is. Pigling takes a dainty bite and totters off.

'What an identity crisis on that guy,' says Benjamin.

'No kidding,' replies Peter. 'Let's go check out my new house.'

Peter and Benjamin head up the path, away from the garden, to Mr. McGregor's now empty house. Peter smiles at his cousin before kicking the door open. It doesn't open and he is sent flying backwards. Benjamin unlatches it and encourages Peter to try again. This time, he succeeds. They stand shoulder to shoulder in the empty house for a moment. They can't believe their luck. The house is huge!

'The garden comes with a free house!' Peter yells out to the other animals. Peter and Benjamin move the party indoors. Just like that, the garden party becomes a house party! Peter and Benjamin make their way out on to the roof. They can't believe how well everything has turned out.

'The McGregors will torment us no more!' Peter calls out into the lush fields from his very own home. He turns back to look at his cousin. They both smile at each other, happy.

The only thing left to do? Dance!

Chapter Four

YOUNG MR. MCGREGOR'S VERY BAD DAY

Meanwhile, in a very large, very beautiful, very crowded city, a young man is making his way along a busy pavement. It's filled with people tapping on their phones, listening to music, riding bikes and hailing double-decker buses. This is London and the man, Thomas McGregor, is walking into a very expensive department store called Harrods. A row of workers are waiting for him in the staff room. It is almost as if McGregor was a general, and these were his troops, if it were a battlefield and not a department store.

'Fifteen minutes until doors open,' says McGregor to his team. 'They're lined up outside waiting to be dazzled. Let's see how prepared we are.' He heads out from the staff room, his employees falling in line behind him. It is inspection time, one of the things McGregor loves best about his job.

McGregor and his team arrive at the toy department. He inspects a doll's house and spots the tiniest wrinkle on a pillow.

'Janelle, if you were a girl who always dreamed of having her own doll's house, what would you think of this?' asks McGregor, his voice stern.

'I would be excited?' says Janelle nervously.

'Not with this ruffled pillow. This is a nightmare!' says McGregor and fluffs the tiny pillow. 'Toss and fluff. Toss and fluff. It's not rocketry. Rocketry is next.' And with that, McGregor heads to the rocketry section. He measures the rockets' angles with a compass.

'82.6 degrees. The angle at which *Apollo 13* was launched. I know you think I'm crazy. But the little girl who wants to be an astronaut is going to know. And we've just blown up her dreams. Like *Apollo 1*,' says McGregor, firmly.

Next, it's the toilets.

'Don't be afraid to really get in there,' McGregor says, kneeling over a toilet and scrubbing away. 'Our toilets should be as clean as a drinking fountain,' he continues and takes out a straw as if he is going to drink the water. The workers watch in horror until a head pops around the toilet door.

'McGregor, the General Manager has asked

to see you.' McGregor freezes just before his straw touches the toilet water.

'This is it. My promotion. They said it could happen this week. How do I look?' asks McGregor.

'Like a man about to drink toilet water with a straw,' says one horrified worker.

'Perfect,' says a distracted McGregor. He straightens his coat and heads off.

McGregor stands looking at the lift's mirrored door, rehearsing what he will say.

'Thank you, ma'am. I will pin the Associate General Manager name tag on my jacket with honour,' says McGregor, before the lift arrives and takes him to the General Manager's floor.

On the way up, Thomas smiles at a pretty customer that gets in the lift beside him. She smiles back as she presses the button and smudges the brass. Quickly, and ever the perfectionist, Thomas rubs off the smudge with his handkerchief. The pretty lady is less than impressed.

'Where were we?' he asks, turning to her.

'Nowhere,' she snaps.

McGregor enters the General Manager's office. He takes a seat at the desk opposite the General Manager herself.

'I have some bad news, Thomas,' says the General Manager.

'No, no. Don't say it,' says Thomas.

'Yes. Your great-uncle has passed away.'

'What?' says McGregor, confused, his mind filled only with thoughts about the promotion.

'I'm very sorry,' the General Manager continues and stands to put a hand on his shoulder.

'What about the promotion?' says McGregor. It's the only thing he cares about right now.

'Excuse me?'

The General Manager is shocked. Surely Thomas McGregor should be more concerned with the death of a family member?

'Associate General Manager. What I've been working towards for the past ten years,' says McGregor, trying to keep the conversation on track.

'You're in shock. I understand. In times of grief –'

'No grief. Did I get it or not?' barks McGregor, interrupting the General Manager before she can go on any more about grief and such nonsense.

'What? No. It went to Bannerman,' says the General Manager.

'Bannerman? The only Bannerman I know is Nigel Bannerman and he's an –'

'That's the one.'

'He's an imbecile! He's not even that.' McGregor can't quite believe what is happening.

'But he happens to be the chairman's nephew. You think I want our best man passed over?' says the General Manager. She's in a very difficult position.

'Then don't pass me over,' pleads McGregor. He won't let this go. 'Overrule the chairman. That would be a gutsy call I would respect. True leadership.'

'Thomas, now's not the time to think about work. Your great-uncle has passed!'

'Whom I never met! Am I to mourn every dead person with my last name?' says McGregor, childishly. This is not how he thought today would go.

'Take as much time as you want,' says the General Manager.

'I don't want time. I want the promotion. I deserve the promotion.'

'I know this is a great blow to you and you have every right to be upset. But I'm begging you, just think of this as a temporary setback and don't do anything rash. And my condolences,' says the General Manager, eager for the conversation to be over.

There is little else to say so the General Manager

shows McGregor out of her office. McGregor seems quite calm and collected as he makes his way back to his beloved toy department. The General Manager peers out, just to make sure everything is OK.

McGregor nods politely at the customers and workers as he walks by. He looks back at the General Manager and gestures, 'I'm fine. All good.' Everything is fine.

McGregor continues to walk through the store. He passes a display case jam-packed with porcelain dolls. He passes another case with glass angels. Nothing. They are lovely, and he is fine. Another case contains a house of cards and, still, McGregor is calm. He does not need a promotion. Really, he is fine.

McGregor then sees someone coming straight towards him. Someone with a dopey look on his face, earrings in both ears and walking around the department store as if he owns the place. His name tag reads 'Bannerman'.

'Good luck, Nigel,' says McGregor as the dopey man comes up to him.

'You know it, my man,' says Bannerman and gives McGregor a fist-bump before walking off.

'Fist-bump?' says McGregor to himself, his voice filled with disgust. He takes a few more steps and then slowly turns back. They chose a man who fist-bumps over him? McGregor can feel the calm slipping away.

McGregor walks by another toy stand, only this time he does not keep going. Instead, he gives the stand a giant knock. It goes flying. In his path, is another toy stand that he also sends flying. And another. McGregor can feel his anger rising and falling with each toy stand he knocks.

But then, there are no more toy stands and McGregor starts knocking over, and throwing, whatever he can get his hands on. That will show them!

McGregor, in a blind rage, is not only having a meltdown in front of customers, but also in front of the Harrods security office who have seen everything via the security cameras dotted throughout the store. The security guards manage to stop McGregor's rampage before he does too much damage. The security guards, accompanied by the General Manager, lead a dazed McGregor out of the store. In his arms is a box full of his personal items.

'This might actually be a blessing in disguise. Get a hobby, learn a language, get some dirt under your fingernails. Get some perspective,' says the General Manager.

'Pfft. You sound like every teacher, friend, employer, family member and vague acquaintance I've ever had,' says McGregor, hardly realizing what has just happened to his life.

'Might I suggest some time in the country? It's calming. Serene,' offers the General Manager, her voice full of concern for her once star employee.

The countryside is exactly what McGregor needs.

In the countryside, specifically, in Old Mr. McGregor's bathroom, Mrs. Tiggy-winkle approaches the toilet.

'Ugh. Some animal left the seat up,' she says with disgust. She puts it down and then . . . drinks out of the toilet bowl. A loud banging on the door interrupts her mid gulp.

'Hold on! Occupied!' she yells.

Back at the party, the animals are still dancing and eating as fast as they can. The fountain is filled with animals laughing, while others slide down the banister before leaping on to, and then off, the chandelier.

The animals are performing an amazing dance routine, led by Pigling Bland.

'I didn't even realize I could dance!' says a very surprised Pigling Bland.

'Certainly didn't realize I knew all the same dance moves as everyone,' says Jemima Puddle-duck.

'Welcome to the new world, where anything is possible,' says Peter, surveying his new, grand manor.

'I can fly!' yells Cotton-tail as she jumps off the balcony and then realizes that, actually, she can't.

Splat!

'Not everything. Cotton-tail, better choices. We talked about this,' says Peter as he moves through the party like the host with the most. 'Good to see you. Thanks for coming. There's no rules. Help yourself to anything. It's all fair game.'

Mopsy is sitting on the couch with an excited Flopsy, who is hopping up and down to the music.

'Look at this pattern. It's stunning,' says Mopsy.

'Come on, let's dance,' says Flopsy.

But Mopsy isn't listening.

'I'm going to make a dress out of it,' says Mopsy.

'Great idea. But not now. Let's dance,' says Flopsy as she drags her sister on to the dance floor just as Peter walks by.

'Peter, dance with us!' says Flopsy.

'Oh no, I'm not much of a dancer,' says Peter, shaking his head.

'Come on!' insists Mopsy.

Peter can't say no to his sisters so he joins in, a bit stiffly. But then something starts to happen.

'Whoa, what's going on? What's happening down there? I'm not even controlling this!' says Peter as he starts to burn up the dance floor. He's a great dancer!

'Let's go get Mum and Dad!' says Peter, excitedly.

'They're dead, Peter,' says Mopsy, a confused look on her face.

'Metaphorically, Mopsy,' explains Peter.

The siblings dash out of the party and return moments later with a portrait of their parents, one that Bea has painted. Flopsy, Mopsy and Cotton-tail try to hang it up on the wall. Peter's instructions aren't helping.

'Higher. To the left. To the right. To the left. More. Too far. Lower. Down. Right. Right. Higher. Higher. Lower. Lower. Up. Right. Down. Up. Left. Middle. Up.'

This is hard! The rabbits give up and leave the portrait where it is.

'Perfect,' Peter says to his sisters before turning back to the portrait of his mum and dad. 'He's gone now, guys. Just wish you were here to enjoy it.'

Chapter Five

TROUBLE IN PARADISE

The sad sound of a violin fills the silence of a very, very neat flat. It can only belong to Thomas McGregor. As he plays his violin, he looks across the street at Harrods. Through the window he can see his precious toy department. He has always loved living so close to where he worked. Until now.

Knock, knock.

McGregor opens the door to find a postman on his delivery round.

'Thomas McGregor? Sign here, please,' says the postman, who checks the return address on the package. 'From Windermere. Fancy place, that. You must know some fancy people.'

'I don't know anyone from Windermere,' says McGregor.

'It's from Unclaimed Property. Usually means you inherited something,' says the postman helpfully and hands the package over. McGregor quickly opens it and sees that it is a will with several pictures of the McGregor manor.

And a key. Thomas has inherited a manor from a great-uncle he never met.

'Windermere. That's out in the country.' Thomas McGregor can't keep the disgust from his voice.

'Fancy country,' says the postman. 'Houses there go for a king's ransom.'

'How rich a country is that king from?' says McGregor, considering his options. An idea is starting to form in his mind. 'Ransom enough to buy my own store?'

'I'd imagine so,' says the postman, leaning against the doorframe.

'And fill it with the finest merchandise?' says McGregor.

'Should do, yes,' says the postman.

'Big enough to have tempered glass shelving and seasonal window decorations?' McGregor can almost see it, his own store.

'That I'd have to do some research on, sir. Can I get back to you mail-time tomorrow?' asks the postman. McGregor's face rearranges into a triumphant smile. When one door closes, another one opens. Thomas decides to take the biggest leap of his life. He is going to the countryside after all.

Thomas's mission takes him to Paddington station. It's one of the busiest stations in London, taking crowds of people to every corner of the country, and beyond. And right in the middle of this crowd are two tiny grey feet. The feet of one Johnny Town-mouse. He is a confident, streetwise mouse dressed in a blue blazer, a shirt and a bright red tie.

'Coming through . . . 'Scuse me, darling. On your left,' says Johnny Town-mouse. He weaves his way under the feet of the bustling commuters making their way through the station. He spots a pretty mouse pulling her suitcase. 'Need some help, love? A pretty mouse like you shouldn't have to carry all that weight. Unless you want to give me . . .'

Shwoop!

Before Johnny Town-mouse can finish flirting with the poor, unsuspecting, pretty mouse, he gets collected by a dustpan wielded by a maintenance man. The girl mouse walks off but, after a minute, Johnny drops right back by her side. His clothes might be dishevelled and covered in rubbish, but he doesn't let that deter him.

'. . . a ride? Where were we?' he continues.

She rolls her eyes and disappears into the crowd. Johnny is unfazed.

'Coming through! Coming through!' he yells, but his voice is drowned out by McGregor's.

'Round trip to Windermere!' says McGregor.

Johnny smiles and jumps into McGregor's bag. That is exactly where he is headed.

The train travels through the city as McGregor finds an empty seat and makes himself comfortable. He is not the only one. Hidden below, Johnny Town-mouse also makes himself comfortable in the mouse compartment. A few other mice are already there, eating and playing cards.

'How's it going, boys? Johnny Town-mouse is in the house. Recognize!' he announces to everyone as he takes off his hat and puts it on what he thinks is a hook. It isn't. The hat falls down into a vent, which sucks it away. Johnny pauses for a millisecond, but powers on.

'Last season's style anyway,' he says. Johnny opens his briefcase and takes out another hat, proud of his fashion-forward thinking.

'Where you diddle-dots headed?' Johnny asks his fellow mice.

'Blackpool. We got a share house on the beach. Gonna be epic,' says a mouse wearing a tracksuit.

'That's cute. But I'm not in playschool any more. My ticket says Windermere,' boasts Johnny.

'Off to visit your grandmother?' asks another mouse, causing all the others to laugh out loud.

'Laugh it up, smooks. I'm headed to the

biggest party of the year. And not just mouses. All kinds. Squirrels, rabbits, *puddle-ducks*,' he says.

Above, McGregor opens a guide book to the Lake District. He flips through the pages just as a woman appears in the doorway to his compartment.

'Are these seats free?' she asks with a smile.

'Of course, please,' says McGregor, a smile appearing on his own face.

'Kids! This way. Hurry up, pile in,' yells the woman as four wild children run up to the seats. They start wrestling and playing video games. One of the children has a cage with two gerbils inside. McGregor's smile quickly turns into a sad frown.

The gerbils in the cage whisper to Johnny Town-mouse, 'Help. Us.'

As dusk falls, the train pulls out of Windermere station leaving McGregor alone on the platform. He doesn't notice that Johnny Town-mouse is standing beside him. Nor does he see the newly freed gerbils standing right beside Johnny. As the train rushes past, Johnny sees the boys on the train, holding the empty gerbil cage. Their mother is furiously looking for their missing pets.

'I can spin around and not touch a wall!' says the first gerbil, still not quite believing he is free.

'Sweet freedom!' says the second gerbil before they both collapse in two dizzy balls.

McGregor grabs his suitcase and makes his way to a taxi. He hands the driver a piece of paper.

'Do you know this place?'

'The McGregor manor,' says the driver, Betty. 'Is that where you're staying?'

'Not staying. That implies it's not temporary, which it is. I'm merely checking the manor's condition before I sell it,' says McGregor.

'So do you want me to take you there or not?'

Behind them, Johnny Town-mouse is listening to their conversation.

'He's going to the same place we are.'

'You're taking us with you?!' says one of the gerbils before they high-five each other.

'He'll ruin the party,' says Johnny. 'I better not have come all this way for nothing.'

'We're going to a party?!' says the other gerbil. Freedom is so exciting!

Johnny signals to the gerbils to climb on to the top of the taxi. It pulls away from the station.

McGregor is very unhappy as he rattles around in the back of the cab as it drives him through the winding country roads of Windermere. Up top, Johnny is smiling at the gerbils as they surf the air with their arms up.

'Just want to let you know, no matter what happens, you've made us the happiest we've ever been in our lives,' says one of the gerbils.

'And don't get freaked out by this, but you're our *Best. Friend. Ever*,' says the second gerbil.

'Means a lot, gerbs. Much love,' says Johnny as he pounds his chest and reaches out to pound the chest of one of the gerbils. This, unfortunately, knocks the gerbil off his feet and he sails off into the night air.

'How far away are we from our destination?' says the gerbil who is left. Maybe freedom is not so great after all.

'Close. It's right over there,' says Johnny and points in the direction of the manor. As he does so, he knocks the other gerbil off his feet and he, too, sails off into the sky.

Inside the McGregor manor, the party that Johnny Town-mouse is so eager to get to has got bigger. The rabbits are flinging carrots at the ceiling like darts, animals play spin the carrot and a hedgehog is having his belly shaved. Peter Rabbit is still the host with the most and the party spirit has definitely taken over.

It's Cotton-tail who first notices something

is wrong. She stops dancing and puts her ear to the ground.

'A man's coming. There's a man coming,' she says.

It's dark when McGregor's taxi pulls into the drive of the manor. He gets out and looks at the old house and its destroyed garden. There are bits of vegetable strewn everywhere, as if they have been pulled from the dirt and eaten by animals. The gate has come off its hinges and clumps of grass are scattered around the garden. It is a mess. The taxi drives off as Johnny Town-mouse leaps from the roof. He runs ahead of McGregor towards the party.

'Get up! The owner's coming,' says Johnny to the animals in the garden. They are jolted out of their party mode. 'That's right. I got all the way out here and the party's about to be shut down. Let's go, chop chop.'

The animals start to scurry out of the manor.

'Owner's coming! Human!' yells Johnny as McGregor walks towards the house.

Thomas does everything he can not to walk on anything nature-related. He'll stick to the paving stones thank-you-very-much. With a little hopscotching, he arrives at the house.

He looks up and sees a shadow pass by the window. That can't be right. The house should be empty now that his great-uncle is dead. McGregor spots a sign. He reads it to check he is at the right address. The sign is dripping with squashed vegetables. McGregor wipes the mush off to reveal the actual word: McGREGOR. Hmmm, it is the right place.

Meanwhile, Johnny continues to run through the manor, warning everyone in sight.

'The owner's outside! Party's over. Usually I start the party, but right now, the party's over. Owner! Human!'

The animals scurry for the exit. Johnny passes three puddle-ducks and he's immediately distracted.

''Sup, ducks. What's quacking?' he says. The puddle-ducks just roll their eyes.

Peter notices the animals disappearing. He spots Johnny Town-mouse, who is busy shouting orders, 'Human! Everyone out! Human!'

The rabbits look out the window and see McGregor in the shadows. They whisper nervously to each other.

'That looks like Mr. McGregor!' says Flopsy.

'But not dead!' says Mopsy.

McGregor makes his way to the front door and puts his key in the lock. The animals scurry away . . . apart from Tommy Brock, who is frozen with fear. The door handle turns, and Peter manages to tackle the badger out of the room just in time.

McGregor appears in the doorway. He takes a step in and feels around for a light switch. As the room brightens, McGregor finally sees the mess he has inherited. The house looks as if animals have been living in it! McGregor cannot believe he would be related to someone who lived in such filth. His uncle must have been a real pig.

Then, without warning, Pigling Bland reveals himself from underneath a sheet on the couch.

'Aaaahhhh!' yells McGregor, his face distorted in fear.

Pigling Bland yelps in response and McGregor jumps just as a crowd of animals rush out past him. He watches, stunned. Then he gathers himself, grabs the coat stand and starts swinging at the animals.

'Get out of my house! Shoo! Vermin!' yells McGregor.

Peter and Cotton-tail slide down the banister and scoot by McGregor. Thomas and Peter lock eyes. It is as if time slows down as McGregor swings the coat stand like his great-uncle used to swing his rake. But this young, strong McGregor is much better at it.

Time speeds up again. Peter runs out of the house with the other rabbits.

'He had the keys!' says Flopsy.

'He's gotta be a McGregor!' says Cotton-tail.

'He's come back to life!' says Mopsy.

'Or he's a different McGregor with similarly evil characteristics!' says a sensible Benjamin.

The bunnies head out and join all the other animals outside, two of whom are the gerbils.

'We made it!' says one of the gerbils as they pass Johnny.

'Party's over. Turn it around,' says Johnny.

The gerbils turn around and get swept away with the other animals, still happy to be part of life outside a cage. Up ahead, a car has stopped. Its headlights are trained on a large deer. The deer is transfixed. He can't move.

'Felix! Blink! Blink!' says Benjamin.

'Headlights,' says Felix, as if he is in a trance.

Benjamin jumps in front of Felix's eyes and yells, 'Blink!'

Thankfully, it works. Felix finally blinks and Benjamin hurries him along, away from the scene of the party, and the new McGregor.

Chapter Six

MAKING NEW FRIENDS

Next morning, the loud crowing of JW Rooster III wakes a tired McGregor.

'. . . The sun came up again! I can't believe it! I thought when I closed my eyes last night that was it! We have another day of this! Woohoo –' crows JW Rooster.

Thomas takes off his sleeping mask and tries to get his bearings. He is no longer in the city. His great-uncle's house is still a mess.

'Ugh. It wasn't a nightmare,' says McGregor sadly, taking in his surroundings.

Peter is also waking up. He heads out of the burrow, putting on his jacket, and sees McGregor at the bedroom window.

'Ugh. It's a nightmare,' he sighs.

Peter watches as McGregor's frown changes to a look of determination. All he has to do is make the house look nice enough to sell and then he can get back to his life in the city.

Thomas begins to hunt around in the cupboards

for cleaning products. Then he snaps on a pair of gloves, turns on some music and gets to work.

Peter and Benjamin look on as McGregor cleans the floors, scrubs the toilets and removes endless hair balls from the bathtub drain. He's in his element as he straightens and tidies the manor and the garden from top to bottom.

'Well, it was good while it lasted. No one can ever take our memories away. Let's just be thankful and reflect on that,' says Benjamin as he picks out some stray fruit from his ears, left over from the party. He looks at it and then eats it. He offers some to Peter. But Peter is furious.

Bea appears; she has been picking wild flowers in the woods.

'Hey sweeties, checking out the new neighbour, huh? Don't worry, he can't be worse than the old crab bucket. Rest his soul. Never know, maybe he's even a good guy,' she says. 'They're not all bad, I promise. I'll go break it down for him: how we all share our land around here.'

Bea gets a clearer look at McGregor. Deciding he's quite handsome, she heads into her cottage. Meanwhile, McGregor continues with his work and re-attaches one of the gates.

'It's all right. We can always go in the . . .'

But before Peter can finish his thought, the new Mr. McGregor races around the garden, almost at hyper-speed, and re-attaches the back gate. It's like he is a superhero. ' . . . back gate. All good. I can still climb over the . . . ' Again, Peter's words trail off as McGregor zooms around the garden. He sets about removing all the farm equipment surrounding the fence. 'Whatever. He'll never find the secret . . .'

McGregor jams a stone in a hidden hole. And then another, for good measure.

'Huh. I never even saw *that* hole,' says Peter.

This new young McGregor has made getting into the garden very, very tricky indeed.

'Hello?' says Bea, just as McGregor is hammering in a stake. She's changed into a sun dress.

McGregor drops his hammer.

'Didn't mean to startle you. I'm Bea,' she says, giving McGregor her best smile. 'I live right over there.' Bea points to her cottage, so McGregor can see exactly how close she lives.

'Thomas,' says McGregor and points far, far away. 'I live way over there. London. I'm just here temporarily. Fixing up this place to sell. I'm going to use the money to open my own toy store. Preferably near Harrods so they can witness their own downfall.' He shakes his head. 'Sorry, I'm just . . . a little out of my element,' explains McGregor.

'Well, I think you'll find this element is pretty fabulous. For my money, it's the most beautiful place on Earth,' says Bea, looking out across the countryside, lost in her thoughts.

'It just got a lot more beautiful,' he says, staring at Bea.

'You didn't just say that. No, you didn't just say that!' She bursts out laughing.

'What? No. Look how perfect that is. Clean, straight, functional,' says McGregor, pointing behind Bea to the perfectly fixed gate.

'Oh. Right. The gate,' says Bea. 'I thought you were saying I was . . .'

'You're beautiful, too. Just not the subject I was on,' says McGregor.

'I'll take it,' says Bea.

'No, I didn't mean – Well, I did mean. Not that I'm – I would never –' McGregor tries, and fails, to get out the right words.

'No, of course you'd think a gate was more beautiful than me. I mean, look at it. Look what it can do,' says Bea as she swings the gate open, and then swings it closed. 'In, out, in, out. What beauty –'

They talk over each other for a minute. And then:

'Thomas,' says McGregor, introducing himself, starting again.

'Bea,' replies Bea.

The rabbits look on as McGregor and Bea smile at each other.

'That's a lot of smiling,' says Flopsy, just as Johnny Town-mouse drops in from the tree above.

'Coming through. Coming through. 'Sup bunnies? Missed you at the after-party last night. It was wicked.' Johnny pauses for a millisecond. 'I kissed a duck. Did I say that out loud? I hope I did, 'cause I wanted you to know it. I kissed a duck.'

Johnny looks very pleased with himself. The bunnies all stare at him. He stares back.

'Tragic it's all over,' Johnny continues, looking at Peter. 'You were about to be legendary, son! You keep this going and the whole kingdom will be chanting your name,' he says, pointing at the garden and all its vegetables. With this new McGregor, there won't be any more animal parties any time soon.

'What's your name, anyway?' asks Johnny Town-mouse.

'Peter Rabbit.'

'Really? Just a regular name and then just what you are? All right. Whatever. In any case, it's through with and you're just a regular rabbit again,' says Johnny.

Johnny heads off as the bunnies turn their attention back to the garden. Bea is tugging on one of the gates. It looks like she is checking its sturdiness.

'These gates are awfully sturdy. Expecting an alien invasion?' Bea asks as she continues to tug on one of the gates.

'Need to keep the wildlife out where they belong,' says McGregor, looking around.

'They actually belong everywhere. It was really their place first. You're familiar with science, yes? We're the latecomers,' explains Bea.

'Are you from here?' asks McGregor. Only country folk talk like that.

'No. But I've been here almost a year and I already feel like it's home,' says Bea.

'If I may, what is it you do out here?' McGregor asks.

'I'm a painter. Portraits mostly. It's going great. Some modern, also surrealism, abstract every now and then. It's going great. It's why I came out here, to really focus on my craft, clear my head, really tap into my creativity. It's going great,' says Bea. She's unsure if she is trying to convince Thomas or herself.

'Sounds like it's going great,' says McGregor.

'It really is,' says Bea.

'I'd love to see them some time.'

'Yeah.' Bea pauses for a moment. 'I was on my way to getting my master's in fine art but decided why hide behind a lecture stand when I should try to see if I can do it myself? Not that teaching isn't an honourable profession.' Bea pauses again to take a breath. 'Anyway, I'd always wanted to see if I had it in me to be one of those artists in my textbooks. I saved up all my money and here I am.'

Bea blushes. She has definitely said far too much.

The rabbits, meanwhile, have crept closer to get a better look.

'That's a lot of words,' says Flopsy.

'Probably telling him to take down the fence and give us back our land,' nods Benjamin.

'And if he doesn't, he'll have to deal with Peter,' says Mopsy.

'Who thinks nothing of killing a McGregor,' adds Cotton-tail.

They watch Bea as she reaches into her bag. Benjamin cranes his head to see what she will pull out. It's a wrapped gift with a bow made of flowers.

'A beautifully wrapped present,' says Flopsy.

'That bow is so pretty,' says Mopsy at the same

time as Flopsy says, 'It's made of chrysanthemums!'

'I brought you a housewarming gift,' says Bea as she hands McGregor the present. 'For bird watching.'

McGregor carefully peels off the wrapping paper. Inside is a pair of binoculars and a notebook.

'I'm not really a bird person. Flying all over. I prefer things in their place.'

'They're in their place. The sky. That's their place,' says Bea.

'Thank you. You didn't have to,' says McGregor.

'I know. Especially since now I know you're leaving straight away,' says Bea, trying to keep her disappointment at bay.

'The quicker I sell, the quicker I can get back to real life.'

'This seems pretty real to me,' says Bea, poking herself to make her point.

McGregor looks through the binoculars. When he scans past the rabbits they dive down, hoping not to be caught.

'I don't see any birds,' McGregor says.

'It's not a kaleidoscope. You have to spot one first,' explains Bea. 'There. A robin redbreast.'

McGregor looks through the binoculars until he finds it.

'Yes! I see it. It has wings!'

'Birds tend to have those,' Bea says. 'It's their

defining characteristic. And you spotted your first one. Mark it down.'

'There's a way of documenting and organizing the chaos of the sky?' says McGregor, still looking through the binoculars, delighted with his gift. As he continues to scan for birds, he passes over the rabbits again. And once more, they dive out of sight.

'See? Real life happens everywhere. It was nice meeting you,' says Bea.

'Yes, you too,' says McGregor.

Bea opens the gate.

'Let's leave this open, huh? For the wildlife.' She smiles and heads off.

As she leaves, McGregor walks out of the garden with his binoculars trained to the sky. Lost in the natural world. Until his binoculars find Bea and he watches her walk away. He's smitten. McGregor starts to think that spending time in the country might not be such a bad thing after all.

Then, something pops up. A brown blur. It's a rabbit. It's five rabbits. McGregor watches as they race towards the other end of the garden. He tries to keep up with them using his binoculars but they are too fast.

Chapter Seven

TRAPPED IN A TRUCK

The rabbits race towards the McGregor garden.

'She did it!' says Mopsy.

'We got it back again!' says Cotton-tail.

'She always comes through for us. I knew she would,' says Peter. The bunnies dart past McGregor, who is still looking through his binoculars, and head for the open gate. But just before they get there, McGregor drops the binoculars and hammers the date closed. He then adds chicken wire at the bottom for good measure. The rabbits screech to a sudden halt, stunned. McGregor takes one last look at his newly secured garden and heads into the house.

'I guess she didn't get her point across,' says Benjamin, sadly. The triplets hang their heads. There is no way they will be able to get into the garden now.

But Peter has other ideas. That mischievous twinkle is back.

'That garden is ours. Nothing has changed.

I'm going in,' he says with a lot of confidence.

'Right behind you,' says Cotton-tail.

Peter puts his paws out and stops her.

'No.'

'But he's blocked all our lookouts. And look at him,' Cotton-tail says. She points towards McGregor who is aggressively hoeing something in the garden. Peter pauses, unsure of himself.

'*I'll* go with you!' says Benjamin, a little too loudly. 'Because you're my cousin, and I'm brave.' Benjamin puffs his chest out to make his point.

Relief washes over Peter's face. The new McGregor is tough and Peter could use all the help he can get. Not that he would ever admit that to anyone.

Benjamin and Peter head off.

'Why does he get to go into the garden?' says Cotton-tail. She is always left in the safety of the sidelines.

Flopsy, Mopsy and Cotton-tail watch as Peter and Benjamin creep towards McGregor's garden. They shimmy their way up a gutter, across a power line and down some plants until they find their way in. McGregor misses it all. He knows something is going on but he can't quite spot it.

Before long, the two rabbits find themselves in front of a row of the juiciest carrots they have ever seen. Sneaking into the garden is always worth it. They are about to take a bite when they are stopped in their tracks.

THWACK!

It is Thomas McGregor. He swings his rake and they take off running. McGregor is just as quick and is soon hot on their paws. Two rabbits and one human race through the garden as if it is an obstacle course. Up and over, around and through, they take care to avoid the barbed wire as they slide and leap and crawl and tumble.

Mopsy is watching the whole thing unfold from the top of the shed. But only because she is standing on Cotton-tail who is standing on poor Flopsy, who grimaces in pain, at the bottom again.

McGregor is nearly on top of Peter and Benjamin when they turn to sprint down a row of vegetables. The labels on some tomato plants are blown out of place. McGregor stops, his chest heaving. He cannot help himself. He tries to ignore it but he cannot. He dashes back to the labels and begins straightening them.

Peter looks over his shoulder and notices McGregor tidying the labels. Finally satisfied, Thomas leaps back to his feet.

Seeing McGregor tidy the labels gives Peter an idea. As he runs, Peter knocks down a row of shovels. Sure enough, McGregor stops to pick them up. It works, and gives them a bit of extra time. The rabbits take off on a stampede of destruction. They knock down a sunflower, and then another.

'No!' shouts McGregor. 'I'm going to put those in the brochure! People love sunflowers.'

Thomas is about to grab the rabbits . . . but they slide under the door of the garden shed. Inside, it is pitch black. But only for a moment before the door busts open. McGregor has caught up with them.

'Do you know what we do with rats in the city?' McGregor says as he catches his breath. 'We exterminate them.'

Peter and Benjamin squish closer together under a plant pot. They are nose to nose. Just then, McGregor grabs their pot and lifts it up. Peter jumps out but Benjamin holds on to the inside for dear life. McGregor puts down the pot and starts after Peter. Suddenly, he sees the pot has sprouted feet and is shuffling out of the door.

Benjamin, in the pot, scurries through the garden, heading for an opening into the flower garden. He is about to go through when THWACK! McGregor hurls his rake like a javelin and slams the gate closed. Benjamin smashes into it, bits of the pot flying everywhere. McGregor has him cornered.

The triplets are now watching from the roof.

'You rats are everywhere!' cries McGregor as he slowly walks towards Benjamin.

McGregor slams a trowel into the fence, pinning Benjamin by his jacket.

'That's the end of you, rah-bbit!' says McGregor, sounding very much like his great-uncle. But unlike his great-uncle, this younger version does not collapse and die. Instead, he marches from the garden, still holding Benjamin.

Peter is crushed! Benjamin's brown jacket is still pinned to the gate. Peter grabs it and puts it on top of his own. He needs to get his cousin back.

McGregor walks towards his house, as Peter joins his sisters.

'He's gonna put him in a pie!' cries Flopsy.

But McGregor doesn't go into the house. He goes to the back of his truck, gets a sack and shoves Benjamin into it. He ties the sack and tosses it, with Benjamin inside, on the passenger seat next to his binoculars.

The rabbits sprint towards the truck, clambering on to the back as it drives off.

Chapter Eight

TROUBLE IN TOWN

Peter is starting to realize that this new, young McGregor is a very big problem. Not only has he taken away the rabbits' garden, he now also has Benjamin in a sack in his truck.

From their hiding place at the back of the truck, Peter and his sisters do everything they can to try to grab Benjamin through the open window but nothing seems to work. Eventually, Peter climbs over the roof, on to the bonnet and opens it up. It flies up, blocking McGregor's vision, and distracting him just long enough for Flopsy and Mospy to grab Benjamin out the side window. McGregor slams on the brakes and the bonnet shuts. He angrily drives off again.

At last, McGregor comes to a stop at a bridge overlooking a stream. He gets out and heads to the side, the brown sack hanging limply in his hand. Can he really do it? Can he really get rid of the rabbit?

McGregor stares at the sack. It's not moving. He pokes at it. He listens but he only hears silence. Oh no. Is it dead already? He didn't really want that to happen, did he? McGregor slowly unties the bag, looks inside and takes out . . . the binoculars that Bea gave him. The rabbits made the switch somehow! Furious, he swings the bag in the air. It flies out of his hand and into the water below.

Back at the truck, Peter and the triplets help Benjamin out of his bag. They look over to McGregor, who lets out a yell that can be heard throughout the land as he heads down to the river.

'Are you OK, big guy? Close one, huh?' says Peter as he helps Benjamin into his jacket.

'I could've been pie'd,' says Benjamin. He has been pretty shaken by the whole episode.

'But you weren't. And what an adventure we had!' says Peter, trying to make Benjamin feel better.

'Your jacket's ripped. I'll make you a new one. I have just the fabric,' offers Mopsy.

'I told you not to go in there,' says Benjamin.

'Let's call it water under the bridge. Oh, sorry. Bad choice of words,' says Peter, feeling a little uncomfortable.

Peter looks away from his cousin and sees McGregor squelch back on to the bridge.

He is soaked from head to toe, but at least he has the binoculars – saved from the stream. The rabbits dart out of his view, and out of his reach, but McGregor just heads to the driver's seat.

'Look at him. Almost feel bad for the guy. Almost,' says Peter as McGregor drives off.

'Turn here. Yup, here's good,' says Peter, acting like a backseat driver. Luckily, McGregor can't hear him. 'New to the area, probably taking the next turn. Just using more fuel. Here we go. And . . . turn.'

But McGregor doesn't turn.

'Whoa, this guy has no sense of direction. There's a nice place to turn this beast around. Now or never,' says Peter, willing the truck to turn.

'Where is he taking us?' says Flopsy.

The truck barrels down the road. Flopsy isn't the only one who is worried. None of them know where McGregor is taking them.

The truck trundles down the main street of town. The rabbits look around, still unsure of their location. They've never seen a town before.

'Is this London? Where's the building that tells the time?' asks Flopsy. The bunnies look at a small digital clock in a storefront as the truck drives past.

'Wow! It's so big,' Flopsy, Mopsy and Cotton-tail say all at the same time.

'And there's the Queen! Everyone curtsey,' says Cotton-tail, catching sight of a Royal Mail box with a crown symbol.

Finally, McGregor pulls into a parking space and the rabbits peek out. They find themselves outside a hardware store.

'What can I do for you?' says a shop assistant. He's wearing a name tag with the name 'Chris' on it.

'I have a vermin problem,' says McGregor. He is not messing around any more.

'Rabbits, I'm guessing,' says Chris.

'How d'you know?' asks McGregor.

'You're the new McGregor. Bea's neighbour,' says Phil, another assistant who comes over to see what all the fuss is about.

'How d'you know?' asks McGregor, still not used to country folk and the way they seem to know everything about everyone.

'You fit the description,' says Phil.

'Of what?' says Thomas, feeling a little indignant.

'Someone who wants to sell his house in a hurry and use the profits to open his own toy store?' says Phil.

'That's incredibly specifically accurate,' says a disbelieving McGregor.

'Just make sure she doesn't find out you're launching those rabbits,' warns Phil.

'She loves them like family.'

'I think she just has a thing for those rabbits,' says Chris.

'So how do I "launch" them?' asks McGregor. He's so eager for the rabbits to be gone that Thomas ignores the fact Bea has a very big soft spot for the vermin that are making his life hell.

'Launch 'em or keep 'em out? Electric fence'll keep 'em out. To launch 'em you'll need some firepower,' explains Chris.

Phil makes the sound of an explosion. A big explosion.

Just then, McGregor sees something out the window. It's his truck and all five rabbits are visible, peeking out from the back.

McGregor barges out of the store and rips the sacks from the back of the truck. But the rabbits are gone. He then tears through everything in his truck, trying to catch those wretched vermin. All the while, he is being watched by the hardware assistants, Chris and Phil.

'Rah-bbits!' yells McGregor into the sky.

But Peter, Benjamin and the triplets are nowhere to be found. Unless you're looking somewhere else. Somewhere covered in darkness except for a narrow shaft of light. The bunnies are towering one on top of each other, and guess who is at the bottom.

They are breathing heavily, knowing they have just got away with their lives. Yet again.

Just then, a small package makes its way through the shaft of light. It gets jammed in between Flopsy's face and the wall. The rabbits have jumped inside a postbox!

'Why am I always on the bottom?' moans Flopsy.

Meanwhile, McGregor charges back into the hardware store. Enough is enough.

'Give me everything you've got.'

'Follow me,' says Phil.

The two men head to the back of the store – after McGregor stops to tidy some of the items on the shelves, of course.

'You really should arrange these in order of colour palette,' he says in his best department store voice.

Back in the postbox, Peter's face peeps from the slot. He looks both ways and then hops out, followed by all the others.

McGregor returns to his truck with an armload of boxes. He dumps them in the back.

'Make sure you keep the explosives separate. You push this, this lights, and these go boom,' says Chris cautiously, holding the remote-control ignitor and detonator.

'I understand the fundamental concepts of basic things. Thank you very much,' says a flustered McGregor.

The truck starts to move. The rabbits are out of sight, standing on the wheel-axle of the truck. As they begin to turn under their feet, Flopsy, Mopsy and Cotton-tail panic a little.

'Just match its speed,' Peter helpfully instructs the others. 'Our natural rabbits' pace should be able to keep up with –'

But before Peter can finish offering his help, the five rabbits shoot out of the back of the truck. They land in a heap against a fence.

'Interesting,' says Peter, rubbing his head.

There is a screeching of tyres and the bunnies look up in time to see McGregor almost hit a couple of pedestrians, who are wearing shoes that are far too shiny for the country.

'Watch it, boxhead!' the man yells while slapping the bonnet of McGregor's truck.

'Leave him alone, babe,' says the woman. 'He's just a country bumpkin.' She has a snooty voice that sounds very much like it is from the city.

'A bumpkin?' McGregor repeats to himself as the couple stalk off. He watches them go before a voice interrupts his thoughts.

'Thomas?' It's Bea on her bicycle.

Peter and the others watch as she and Thomas start talking and smiling at each other. Peter can't help but look from Bea to McGregor and back to Bea. What is happening? Why are they smiling like that?

McGregor opens the truck door and gets out. He puts Bea's bike in the back next to the boxes.

'Oh no, he's stealing her bike!' says Benjamin in alarm.

But then, McGregor opens the truck door.

'Oh no, he's stealing her!' says Benjamin in even more alarm.

But Bea is smiling as she gets in.

'Oh no, she's going willingly and seems to be enjoying his company!' says Benjamin. He's more alarmed than he has ever been.

Peter watches with hardened eyes as his sworn enemy and the woman who is a part of his family become friends. Thomas gets back into the truck and starts the engine.

'Come on,' Peter says, unable to keep the hurt from his voice. The rabbits jump into the back of the truck, hiding themselves under the sacks.

The truck heads towards McGregor's manor. Bea and Thomas continue to chat the whole way home.

'That's a lot of smiling. More than before even,' says Flopsy as the rabbits watch the two humans from the back of the truck.

'She is showing more teeth,' adds Cotton-tail.

'Must mean she likes him,' says Mopsy.

'Awww,' say the triplets at the same time.

'No awww,' Peter cuts in. 'She doesn't like him. She's just really nice. She smiles at us all the time.'

Bea gives McGregor a smile that the rabbits have never seen before.

'Not like that, she doesn't,' says Benjamin.

Peter looks back at Bea and the new McGregor. Peter does not like what is going on. Now, he just has to figure out how to stop it.

Chapter Nine

NEW BEST FRIENDS?

The truck stops outside Bea's cottage. McGregor and Bea head inside. The rabbits jump out of the truck and shimmy up the side of the cottage, eager to listen in. They land with a light thud on the glass roof of Bea's conservatory. The rabbits want to see everything that is going on between their beloved Bea and McGregor.

'Would you like something to drink?' Bea asks McGregor.

'Yes, thanks. Are these yours?' McGregor points to the paintings scattered around the room.

'Yes, but they're not very good,' says Bea, rushing over to try to cover the painting that McGregor is looking at.

'This is beautiful. What a majestic mountain,' he says, tilting his head.

'It's an old woman in a hat,' says Bea, correcting him.

'Ah, yes. I see,' says McGregor. He tries but is having trouble seeing the woman, or the hat.

'What about these?' he asks, when he notices Bea's paintings of rabbits.

'Oh, that's just for fun. It's what I paint to avoid working on my real stuff,' says Bea.

'These . . . these are wonderful,' says McGregor as he looks through the stack of bunny paintings.

'You don't have to say that,' says Bea. She finds it difficult to accept compliments about her work.

'It just shows how good they are if I like them, given how much I hate rabbits. Somehow, you manage to make them not look like the vermin they are.'

'You think rabbits are vermin?' asks Bea. She really hopes Thomas is joking. It would be terrible if he hated rabbits!

'Yes. That was a joke. I'm hilarious. And whimsical,' says McGregor hastily. He doesn't want Bea to stop smiling at him.

'Rabbits are perfect creatures. They're generous. Honest. Pure. You should see the way they act towards each other. They do this incredible thing when they're apologizing.'

'Apologizing? Rabbits apologize?' Thomas does not believe it. How can rabbits apologize?

'They're very emotional, intuitive little things. They put their heads together like this.' Bea puts her forehead on McGregor's forehead.

'Anyway,' says Bea, breaking eye contact. 'You'll see. You'll grow to love them.'

She pours out some blackberry spa water.

'I'm allergic to blackberries,' says McGregor, dragging his eyes from Bea's beautiful face to stare at the glass in front of him. 'My throat swells up, I get all purple and blotchy. Like an actual blackberry.'

'Well, we don't want that to happen,' says Bea, taking out the berries and tossing them in the rubbish. Peter can't believe it. Those were delicious-looking blackberries! He lunges at the window but Benjamin grabs him and holds him back.

Bea refills Thomas's glass and his hand brushes against hers. Bea and Thomas look at each other and smile.

The next day, McGregor and Bea hire a rowing boat and glide across a dazzling lake. The pair can't stop smiling at each other, laughing together and holding hands. Later, Bea rides her bike with McGregor balanced in the front basket. They both look deliriously happy. All the rabbits can do is watch sadly from a nearby wall.

A day later Bea and McGregor are sitting by the lake playing BananaGrams™. Each is just as good as the other at using their letter tiles.

McGregor is halfway through telling Bea about his childhood.

'. . . my parents died and I had to move into a group home. That's why I never knew my great-uncle.'

'That must've been traumatic. Did you deal with it OK?'

'Didn't affect me in the slightest,' says McGregor. He's moved all the tiles into a perfectly straight line.

'I can see that,' says Bea, not entirely convinced. Thomas notices his tiles have spelled out ALONE, ABANDON, MUMMY, WHY, BROKEN and HELP.

'I may have some tendencies,' he acknowledges.

'We all have tendencies,' replies Bea, kindly.

'Yeah? What are yours?' says McGregor. Looking at her, Thomas can't imagine Bea being anything other than perfect.

'I guess I have a hard time with people who aren't who they say they are,' says Bea.

'You must hate Halloween,' Thomas smiles.

'It's more about me. I keep calling myself a painter, but I can't finish anything real. I think it might be time to face up and go back to real life,' she says.

McGregor pokes himself in the arm.

'Seems real enough to me.'

Bea smiles at him, at his lovely face, his lovely smile, his lovely hair. He is just . . . lovely.

'We all have a place where we belong in this world. Some of us are just luckier than others in finding it,' says Bea. 'Bananas!'

'Nooooo!' says Thomas, he's not happy that it looks like Bea has won the game. He checks her tiles,

'Is "taradiddle" a word?' he asks, doubtfully.

'Yes. A fib. Pretentious nonsense,' Bea replies.

'That's exactly the definition you'd make up for a made up word!' says Thomas.

'Mr. McGregor. Are you accusing me of taradiddling?' says Bea, laughing.

The rabbits watch as, over the next few days, Bea and McGregor begin to fall in love. The bunnies don't want to believe it, but it's obvious.

One afternoon, Peter decides to take action. When the heavens open and sheets of rain soak through everything, Bea and McGregor make a dash for cover. Safely inside the cottage, the door bangs shut. Peter, the triplets and Benjamin are left outside: cold, wet and feeling neglected.

Drenched and miserable, the rabbits peer through the window. Bea is using her fluffiest towel to dry McGregor's hair. Peter can't believe it. That's his towel! Peter's eyes narrow on McGregor, the man who is slowly taking Bea away from them.

Peter continues to stare longingly into the cottage. Bea heads into the kitchen, leaving McGregor alone in the glass conservatory. The towel is still draped over his head. Thomas can't see through the towel, he's completely blind. This is the time for Peter to make his move. He pushes his way through the door and runs full speed at an unsuspecting McGregor. Just as Peter is about to hit his target, two hands swoop down and pick him up.

'Sweetie! I haven't seen you in forever,' says Bea, back from the kitchen, as she hugs our hero.

McGregor pulls the towel from his face so he can see what is going on. He is very surprised to see Peter in Bea's arms.

'Say hello to my friend, Thomas. He really is much better than the old one,' Bea whispers into Peter's ear.

'Wanna hold him?' she asks McGregor.

'Very much so,' says McGregor with a smile plastered to his face. Bea hands Peter to McGregor, who holds the rabbit at arm's length, like someone would hold a baby who has just pooped everywhere. It doesn't look very comfortable for McGregor or Peter.

'Aw, my two boys are getting along. Nothing could make me happier,' says Bea, smiling. She doesn't notice how uncomfortable Thomas and Peter look in each other's company. 'I need to paint this.'

She rushes from the room, leaving Peter in McGregor's hands. Rabbit and human eye each other up and down, as if they are two boxers about to get into the ring.

'You're mine now, rah-bbit!' McGregor says slowly, staring at Peter. Peter stares back.

Before they know what is happening, the pair start wrestling with each other. They hurtle across the room until Bea walks back in. Then they quickly force themselves into a pose much like a father playing with his son. Peter is on McGregor's shoulders, legs wrapped around his neck. Bea smiles, happy to see her boys getting along.

'Thomas, are your eyes cobalt or winter blue?' asks Bea.

'Winter blue,' says McGregor as he catches his breath.

Bea leaves the room, and it's on again. McGregor swings a nearby mop, narrowly missing Peter once, then twice. The third strike sends Peter flying. He lands on a wheely chair that hurtles straight at McGregor. Peter takes a deep breath and leaps into the air. He snatches the mop from Thomas's hands and in the same swoop hits him on the bottom. McGregor falls to the ground and Peter bounces about the room before landing on his face. The two arch enemies shove and push and pull.

From outside the cottage, Benjamin and the triplets are watching the fight unfold. They cheer when Peter lands a blow, and wince when he doesn't. There's a lot of cheering and wincing going on.

Back inside the cottage, McGregor flings Peter to the ground and lands on top of him like a wrestler. Peter manages to wriggle his way free and finds himself on top of McGregor this time. But McGregor will not be stopped. He squishes Peter up against the window with his bottom just as Bea comes back into the room with some paint. She looks at her best boys and sees that they are cuddling.

'How sweet.' She smiles in their direction.

'Yes. Isn't it sweet?' McGregor says through gritted teeth.

'See? They're not vermin. I could never like

anyone who doesn't like my rabbits,' says Bea, before leaving the room again.

Peter bites McGregor's hand and is free at last. He propels himself once more around the ceiling lamp and back at McGregor. But Thomas catches the rabbit and throws him down on to the table, pinning Peter to the table with a wet paint brush. A wet paint brush that now smears wet paint across one of Bea's in-progress paintings.

'What's going on? My painting!' says Bea suddenly, looking from her ruined canvas to Peter who is standing next to it, with the wet paint brush in his paw.

'You know how uncontrollable wildlife can be,' says McGregor, shaking his head as if he is very disappointed with Peter.

Bea hurries over and shoos Peter out.

'Shoo! Bad rabbit. Shoo.'

Shoo?! Peter can't believe it. He looks back to see McGregor smiling slyly at him.

'I know you like them, but really, they're *animals*,' says McGregor, shaking his head sadly.

Bea doesn't respond. She just closes the door in Peter's face. The slam echoes in Peter's mind as he hangs his head, crushed.

'Did you just get shoo'd?' says Cotton-tail in disbelief.

Peter joins his family back outside, in the pouring rain.

'It looks like he's getting pretty cosy with her,' says Benjamin.

But Peter isn't interested in how cosy they look. Peter is only interested in one thing.

'He's gotta go.'

Chapter Ten

A RABBIT'S REVENGE

The next morning JW Rooster III wakes everyone up. He can't believe it's a whole new day.

'You have got to be kidding me! Again? How long does this sweet life last? Everybody wake up! You're not going to believe this!'

The rabbits all walk across the field, their battle faces on. They are cool and they are tough. They are ready for anything. Peter has them all stretch before they run sprints. Flopsy is always last across the line, as usual.

Then it's time for an obstacle course. The rabbits crawl, hop, roll and fight their way through the challenges, even practising how to set and avoid traps. Flopsy is, again, always last across the finish line.

The training doesn't stop there. Peter constructs five life-size dummies of McGregor. The rabbits each take up a catapult and small pebbles. They all hit their target, except Flopsy. Her first pebble goes this way. Her next pebble goes that way. Her third pebble goes way over there. Poor Flopsy.

'It's OK, Flopsy. You can carry the pebbles,' says Mopsy.

Flopsy, not happy with Mopsy's offer, turns her catapult towards her sister. It misses Mopsy by a mile. Poor Flopsy. A flock of sparrows flies across the sky. They are quickly knocked down by one of Flopsy's shots. Still, the training carries on.

As the bunnies continue to shoot and pummel the dummies, Benjamin walks up to Peter.

'Traps, slingshots. You sure you know what you're doing?'

'We're getting our garden back,' says a determined Peter.

'Is that really what this is about? She's not going to love us any less if she's with him,' says Benjamin. It's like Benjamin can see exactly what is going on in his cousin's head – and heart.

'What are you talking about?' asks Peter. He would never admit to such things. 'Just let me handle this.'

'You know we'll do anything for you, Peter. But just remember what that means,' says Benjamin, looking over at Peter's sisters. Peter follows Benjamin's gaze. The girls are giving it their all, attacking the dummies like mad dogs.

Peter realizes he is putting his family at risk.

'I got this,' he says. He won't, he can't, let anything bad happen to them.

Benjamin sighs.

As morning continues to break across the countryside, the rabbits sneak into the McGregor manor. More specifically, into Thomas McGregor's bedroom. Peter, Benjamin, Flopsy, Mopsy and Cotton-tail stand at the foot of McGregor's bed. They all stare at him. Peter's eyes gleam with determination.

McGregor stirs and groggily opens one eye. He sees that there are rabbits at the end of his bed. That can't be right. He opens the other eye. Yep, rabbits. RAH-BBITS! McGregor rushes to get up and SNAP! His hands get caught in rabbit traps. It is very painful, and not the best way to wake up at all.

Thomas jumps out of bed. His feet hit the floor, landing right on a perfectly placed garden hoe that smacks him in the head. McGregor then steps on a rake. Ouch! He then steps on another hoe. So painful! Then a shovel and it is all too much!

McGregor clutches at his throbbing head. He tries to balance himself.

'Rah-bbits!'

McGregor stumbles into the bathroom to try and wash away his painful morning. He splashes water on his red, sore face and looks in the mirror to see the damage. Except the mirror is covered in steam from the hot water. McGregor rubs it clean. And there is Peter Rabbit! Right behind him. It is just like a horror film.

McGregor spins around and tries to lunge towards the rabbit who has made his morning hell. But instead he slips and crashes to the ground.

SNAP!

McGregor yelps out in pain. He slowly staggers back up. There is a rabbit trap on his head, and Peter is long gone.

'He's gotta go,' says Thomas in a low growl.

McGregor creeps to the window. He waits for Bea to leave so she won't see what he has in store.

As Bea peddles off from her cottage, McGregor races out to his truck. Those rabbits will be sorry they ever set traps in his house!

Meanwhile, in the burrow, while Mopsy is sewing new clothes from all the flowery material she has swiped from the manor, Peter Rabbit is hunched over the earth. He's drawing out detailed battle plans, while Benjamin and Cotton-tail look on.

'His face was so classic! "Aaaaah!"' Peter mimics the panicked look on McGregor's face. 'We got him just where we want him. Now, to the next phase.'

Suddenly, Cotton-tail puts her ear to the ground.

'Something's happening,' she says.

The rabbits run out of the burrow to see what is going on. It is McGregor. He is installing an electric fence system all around the garden. The rabbits are not the only ones watching. Pigling Bland, Tommy Brock and Mrs. Tiggy-winkle are also there.

'Electronic fence. This new generation with their technology,' says Pigling Bland, shaking his head sadly.

'What's he doing to it?' asks Tommy Brock as McGregor spreads peanut butter on the wires.

'Baiting it,' says Peter, with a frown. McGregor was not supposed to fight back. This fence is not part of Peter's plan.

The animals watch as a fly lands on a particularly gooey mound of peanut butter. The fly explodes.

'Well, I want a taste,' says Mrs. Tiggy-winkle, her eyes dancing with delight at the explosion. She marches over to the fence as the animals look on. McGregor is watching events unfold, too. Mrs. Tiggy-winkle stands up and sniffs at the peanut butter before giving it a lick.

ZAP!

Mrs. Tiggy-winkle goes flying! Not only that, her clothes burst off and her spines blast into all the animals.

The animals all scurry away. A smile creeps across McGregor's face. He is very happy with his new fence. It will definitely keep out those annoying rabbits.

Peter realizes he now has to revise his battle plan.

'Remember what Dad used to say to us? "You can't outrun a fox, so use his speed against him."'

'He spoke in riddles? Cool. I wish I knew him better,' says Flopsy.

'What did you have in mind?' says Benjamin, a worried look on his face. What is Peter up to now?

Back at McGregor's manor, Thomas smiles as he opens up his post. Inside is a fancy brochure of the manor, the perfect second home for a city-dweller. Then he looks at a copy of *Department Store*

Quarterly and spots a photo of the dopey-looking Bannerman. Underneath it reads, 'Nigel Bannerman gets coveted position at Harrods'. McGregor fist-bumps the photo.

Suddenly, something catches his eye. He picks up his binoculars and scans the garden. McGregor's smile grows wider when he spies Peter and Benjamin at the fence.

Peter and Benjamin are at the edge of the garden and hop towards the electric fence. McGregor leans forward.

The bunnies grab on to the fence and McGregor winces, waiting.

'Zap,' he says.

Only there is no zap. There are no sparks. There is no explosion. Nothing. Benjamin starts gnawing his way through the wire, while Peter climbs right over it. The smile on McGregor's face disappears. Why is the electric fence not working? It should be keeping the rabbits out, not letting them back in! And soon enough, all five rabbits start swinging on the fence like it is a climbing frame. They lap up all the peanut butter and march into the garden like they own the place.

'No! What is happening?!' yells McGregor.

He runs to the back door and grabs hold of the doorknob.

ZAP!

McGregor goes flying on to the ground. He lies on his back. He is completely stunned and bewildered. Did he just get an electric shock? He stumbles up to the door again and nervously reaches out for the doorknob.

Those clever rabbits have somehow managed to re-direct the powerful electrical current back towards the house and McGregor. Everything he touches shoots horrible shocks up his arm.

ZAP!

McGregor is again blown back. He looks out of the window. He can see Peter and Benjamin feasting on his vegetables. This is not how the plan was supposed to go! McGregor shakes himself off. He then turns on the kitchen taps and splashes some water on his face. He does not make the mistake of reaching for the doorknob again. This time he reaches to open the window.

ZAP!

McGregor cannot believe it! Somehow the entire manor has been electrified, just like the fence was supposed to be.

The rabbits watch as the lights dim on and off inside the manor while the electric current surges throughout the house. The wires have been redirected from the fence to the house.

Inside the house, McGregor stumbles up to the second floor. He is hoping that the windows will not be electrified this high up. McGregor slowly reaches out to one of the windows. When he touches it, he does not get an electric shock. Relieved, McGregor pulls open the window and climbs out on to the roof.

'Rah-bbits!' he yells, grabbing hold of the gutter so he can climb down and get rid of the vermin once and for all.

But McGregor has not learned his lesson. No sooner does he touch the metal pipe than, ZAP!

Thomas blasts off the house and falls into the corn stalks below. He is too stunned to say anything.

'And that should do it. For sure, this time,' says Peter, grinning. 'Shoo.'

Chapter Eleven

NO MORE MR. NICE GUY

McGregor opens his eyes. It is dark. Very dark. There is no power anywhere. It appears he is outside. He gets up and stares at the burrow before marching into the shed.

Moments later, McGregor is back outside with a headlamp around his forehead. In his arms is a box. He walks away from the shed, past the manor and past the garden. He only stops when he reaches the burrow.

Inside, the rabbits are sleeping peacefully after a day of showing McGregor just who is boss in this part of the countryside. But then a red stick lands on the dirt floor of the burrow. Then another. And another. More keep tumbling in, all attached to each other by a long wire. One of them hits Benjamin, who wakes with a jump. When he sees what has woken him up, his eyes go very, very wide. A collection of red explosive sticks is now inside the burrow. Inside their home.

McGregor is kneeling beside the entrance to

the burrow. He dumps the whole box of explosives down the entrance to the burrow, followed by the detonator.

The rabbits are now fully awake. They hold on to the ceiling and wait for the explosion to come.

Pleased with his efforts, McGregor stands up with the remote control in his hand. One quick press of the button and the burrow will explode. BOOM! McGregor smiles. For, you see, McGregor has assumed the bunnies are *not* in the burrow at this very moment.

'Thomas! What are you doing over there?' Bea calls from outside her cottage.

McGregor looks up and scrabbles around for something to say. He definitely cannot tell Bea what he is really up to. That he is about to blow up the burrow.

'Picking wildflowers!' McGregor calls out. 'There's one that looks effervescent in moonlight!'

Thomas yanks some flowers out of the ground and makes his way over to Bea's cottage, pocketing the remote control as he goes.

Carefully, the rabbits try not to touch any part of the floor as they make their way around the room towards the exit. They form a rabbit chain and help each other out to safety. As they leave the burrow and look about into the night, they see a floating headlamp outside Bea's cottage. It is attached to McGregor. The person who has just tried to blow up their home. The headlamp, and McGregor, head inside with Bea and the rabbits follow.

The cottage is filled with candles. It is all very romantic. The rabbits watch as Bea kisses the man who has just tried to blow them up.

'OK, so he's snookered her. We just have to un-snooker her,' says Peter, determined to get Bea away from McGregor once and for all.

'Yeah! Wait, what?' says Cotton-tail.

'We show her the real him. The guy who's been trying to kill us. She sees that, she'll shoo *him*,' says Peter, happy with his new plan.

'Exactly. Wait, did we train for this?' asks Flopsy.

'It's exactly what we trained for,' replies Peter.

'Right. Wait, which part?' says Mopsy, confused.

'Just follow my lead,' says Peter, beckoning for the rabbits to follow.

'He's got this,' says Benjamin, confidently.

The next morning, McGregor is woken by a loud THWUMP. Then a SPLAT. It's fruit at the window.

He is getting sick and tired of waking up to the annoying sounds of the country, and those pesky vermin.

Thomas is about to get out of bed but he stops and checks for traps first. Thankfully the room seems clear, so he gets out of bed.

Another THUMP.

McGregor goes to open the window, then stops. Carefully, he uses his top to test it first to see if it will give him an electric shock. It doesn't. He opens the window and sticks his head out. All the bunnies are in the garden, shooting fruit.

'Rah-bbits!' yells McGregor, noticing that the electric fence has been taken down.

McGregor races downstairs and opens the front door. He then charges into the garden and jumps over the gate. McGregor grabs his hoe and is just about to run the rabbits out of his garden once and for all when a voice stops him in his tracks.

'Morning, Thomas!' says Bea. She steps outside from her cottage, holding a paintbrush in one hand.

McGregor screeches to a halt.

'Yes! Give him everything!' yells Peter.

The rabbits sling all the vegetables and fruit

they have at McGregor. He tries his best to ignore them and talk to Bea.

'Morning!' he says, trying not to engage with the rabbits or their fruit.

THWAP! SPLAT! THUNK!

'Lunch later?' asks Bea, too far away to see what the rabbits are doing to Thomas.

'That would be wonderful!' says McGregor as more fruit lands.

'OK then! See you later!' says Bea. As she's about to go back inside, she remembers something else. 'Red or white wine?'

THWAP! CLUNK!

'Either one!' says McGregor, dodging a tomato.

'You choose!' says Bea.

'White!' yells McGregor as fruit lands on his face.

Peter and the rabbits are making progress, they can just feel it. McGregor will crack at any moment, right in front of Bea!

McGregor turns to stare at the rabbits as Bea heads back inside her cottage. He needs to calm down and think calm thoughts. The rabbits all look at Peter. That did not go to plan at all. McGregor was supposed to get angry in front of Bea, so she could see the real him!

'Blackberries,' says Peter, suddenly.

The bunnies race to the blackberry bush and grab one scraggily berry each. They begin throwing them at McGregor with real gusto. Thomas cleverly ducks and dodges each one. The berries sail past their mark. Flopsy, though, still has hers. She rears back with all her might while Mopsy motions for Flopsy to aim wide right.

Flopsy lets the blackberry go and it flies right down McGregor's open mouth. Flopsy did it! She jumps up and down in delight as Mopsy cheers her on.

'Blackberry,' McGregor gasps and clutches his throat. He starts to turn red and choke. He staggers, unable to breathe, and drops to his knees. McGregor stares at Peter and the others and they laugh back in his face, willing him to react. What's he going to do about it?

Quickly, McGregor takes out his Epi-pen and stabs himself in the thigh. Adrenaline surges through his body.

'Aah!' he says as he sucks in lungfuls of air, beautiful, beautiful air. Then his face darkens.

'That's it!' McGregor charges into the garden, right through the gate and right back out of the garden, and across the way.

The rabbits watch as a determined McGregor heads straight for the burrow. Oh dear!

McGregor pulls the explosives out of the burrow's entrance and marches back towards the manor. He's furious and drops some in his anger, including the one that has the detonator attached to it.

Peter watches and smiles. McGregor is losing it. Bea will soon see the sort of man he is.

'And we've got him,' says Peter, turning to the others, 'Remember your training.' The rabbits all scamper away.

McGregor charges into the garden and into the shed. He emerges with his lighter and sets about lighting one of the red stick explosives before tossing it into one of the vegetable patches.

BOOM!

A cauliflower explodes in front of the rabbits. They dive out of the way.

BOOM! An aubergine explodes next.

BOOM! BOOM! BOOM!

Three corn cobs shoot off their stalks like fireworks. The battle is on.

'She'll be here in no time,' says Peter, rubbing his paws together.

What Peter and the others don't know is that Bea will not be there any time soon because she cannot hear anything. Bea is busy painting and listening to some calming music. The tunes completely drown out the sound of the shouting and the exploding vegetables.

The rabbits fight back. Peter finds a clean shot of McGregor.

'Now,' he calls.

The rabbits start attacking McGregor with any vegetables that he has not yet blown up. He staggers to the ground but still manages to light another explosive. The rabbits' eyes go wide as a rain of fire falls from above them.

BOOM! A cabbage explodes. The rabbits dive for cover. Then a bunch of radishes. Shards of vegetables explode everywhere as the rabbits try to avoid the shrapnel.

Next, a green leafy vegetable explodes and hits Peter right in the mouth.

'Ptfff. Ugh. Kale,' he says as he spits it out.

Benjamin takes a clear shot at McGregor with a stalk of Brussels sprouts. The sprouts hit their target and explode in his face like a grenade.

'Nice, Benjamin!' says Peter.

'Doesn't mean I approve!' Benjamin replies. 'Why isn't she here yet? How could she not have heard all this?'

Bea is still listening to music while painting a portrait that seems to get worse with each brush stroke. She has no idea about the vegetable battle happening outside. And the assaults continue as McGregor lights more explosives and the rabbits throw more vegetables.

Animals have come from everywhere to watch the fight unfold. Pigling Bland, Tommy Brock, the squirrels and Mrs. Tiggy-winkle look from one side of the battle to the other, munching on corn like it's popcorn.

'I'm hit!' shouts Flopsy suddenly.

'Flopsy, noooo!' says Mopsy, turning to her sister in horror. Flopsy's fur is covered in red. Flopsy gives it a lick.

'It's just a beetroot! I'm fine! This is getting quite scary, Mopsy,' says Flopsy.

'I know. But Peter knows what he's doing, right?' Mopsy looks across the battlefield as explosions, hand-to-hand combat and flying vegetables are launched across the garden. Then, a plum flies into the shed window. The gerbils are bunkered inside, shaking and shell-shocked.

'I want to go back to the cage,' says one of the gerbils.

'Let's find a pet store. We're not built for freedom,' says the other gerbil. They hold each other tight, take a deep breath, and make a dash across the battlefield to the other side.

Benjamin is worried for the triplets.

'I'm getting the girls out of here!' he yells at Peter above the noise.

'No! Trust me! She'll come! I got thi–' But before Peter can finish, his face gives him away. He's worried this time, really worried.

Chapter Twelve

BEA TO THE RESCUE

Inside Bea's cottage, Bea is not happy with her work. As the song ends, she begins to beat her painting into submission with a hammer. She stops for a rest and it is then that she can faintly hear something going on outside. The noise seems at odds with the peace and quiet of the countryside.

Outside, McGregor, who is covered in bits of vegetables and fruit juices, spots Peter who is about to throw a head of lettuce. As Peter lets the lettuce fly, McGregor swings his rake. It connects with the lettuce. The lettuce is sent flying back towards Peter. Knocked flat on to the ground, Peter has no time to catch his breath before McGregor leaps on top of him. He is pinned by the throat with the rake.

'What is going on?'

It is Bea to the rescue. Again. Everyone stops and whips their heads in unison towards the sound of her voice. Peter wriggles out from under McGregor's rake.

'Just making sure he's OK!' McGregor says, covering up for the fact that he wished Peter very much was *not* OK.

'Why? What happened?' Bea looks at Peter, her eyes filled with concern.

'Little guy choked on a radish. Bit off more than he could chew, I'm afraid. But I saved him,' says Thomas, while he smacks Peter on the back. Repeatedly. 'You OK, little fella? Yeah, that's right. Breathe. That's it.'

'Did I hear explosives?' Bea asks, looking around for evidence of the noise she thought she had heard.

McGregor shakes himself out of battle mode and walks over to Bea. Peter and the others run behind him. They cannot wait to see what Bea will do when she realizes what McGregor has done.

'No, no. I was just doing some weeding,' says McGregor in his most charming voice.

Peter and the others exchange looks. This cannot be happening again. Then Peter notices something on the ground. It's the remote control. It must have fallen out of McGregor's pocket.

'Because some people around here have taken to explosives to keep the rabbits out,' says Bea, frowning at the chaos all about her.

'What? I can't even imagine that. They're angels!

Is that a broad-shouldered nuthatch?' McGregor says, distracting Bea by pointing to the sky.

'No. It's a wagtail. See the crown?' They both look as the bird sails overhead.

McGregor leads Bea out of the garden as Peter looks around in disbelief. He spots the line of explosives McGregor dropped as he marched from the burrow to the garden. Then, Peter sees the explosive with the detonator attached to it. If he presses the remote control, Bea will finally see what sort of person McGregor is. A person who uses explosives on her beloved rabbits. And so Peter does it. He presses down on the remote control.

BLAM! It explodes.

'You are using explosives! You lied to me!' says Bea. Her eyes fill with angry tears.

'Yes, but, no –' McGregor starts to explain but Bea cuts him off.

'I can't believe you!'

Peter smiles, his eyes sparkling with mischief. He did it. Finally, Bea sees exactly who McGregor is. At long last, the rabbits will have Bea back to themselves.

Cotton-tail sidles up to her brother. She can't believe he managed to do it. Yes!

BLAM!

There's another explosion, ignited from the first blast. Then another. BLAM!

And yet another stick explodes. The rabbits all look towards the ruined field. Peter's smile fades away as he realizes what is about to happen. The trail of explosives leads back to the burrow, their home. The sticks continue to send dirt and grass flying everywhere. The explosions are getting closer and closer to the rabbits' home.

BLAM! BLAM! BLAM! BLAM!

And then they stop. The rabbits and humans begin to relax. Silence begins to settle over the battle-weary animals when there is one, big, final . . .

KABLAM!

Smoke, fire and clouds of dirt shoot from under the trees until there is a loud snapping sound. It's the fir tree that stands very near Bea's house. snapping at its base. The fir tree falls, and falls, and falls. It lands with a very loud crash. Right on top of Bea's glass conservatory, smashing it to pieces.

'Whoa,' says Mrs. Tiggy-winkle as one of her spines flies off.

'My house!' cries Bea as McGregor and the bunnies look on in horror.

Peter can't believe what has just happened.

He didn't mean to ruin beautiful Bea's beautiful cottage. He quickly shoves the detonator into the pocket of his jacket.

'He detonated it! He pushed the button!' It's McGregor pointing the finger at Peter.

'He's a rabbit!' says Bea, angry at Thomas for blaming the rabbits, angry at the explosives for ruining the tree and even more angry at the tree for ruining her home.

But McGregor will not be stopped. He has to make Bea see that he is not the one to blame. That it was her precious rabbits all along.

'He can do a lot of things, Bea. A lot of things. They're devils. Stealing from the garden, electrocuting me,' McGregor tries to explain. 'And traps! They booby-trapped my house with traps! On my head! Like a prisoner! They shot me off my house!'

'You've lost your mind,' says Bea, shaking her head.

'I'm so sorry,' says McGregor.

'I can't believe I thought I liked you.'

'You did! And I liked you! I like you!' McGregor can see Bea pushing him away.

She walks over to the rabbits, who all look very, very guilty. They never meant for Bea, or her house, to get hurt.

'Are you OK, sweeties?' asks Bea, full of concern for her friends.

'It was an accident! I can fix this!' McGregor will not give up.

'Some accident. I should have you arrested. For what you did, and for lying to me.' The look of hurt on Bea's face is unbearable for McGregor to see.

'You don't really mean that,' he says, scrambling for the words that will make everything better.

'I do. I mean what I say. Which is more than I can say for you,' says Bea. She looks at the rabbits. 'Come on. Let's get away from this evil man.'

Bea and the rabbits walk off. But McGregor can't let Bea just walk away. He calls after her, 'Wait! Let me explain!'

But it's too late. She's gone.

The next morning, a silence blankets the countryside in the wake of the battle for McGregor's garden. JW Rooster III breaks the silence,

'. . . No way! The sun came up again. Woohoo! More of this! Although things aren't going so great *now,* maybe last night should have been it!'

A 'FOR SALE' sign has been placed in front of the gate. Everything has changed.

Inside the destroyed burrow, the rabbits are all awake. They are still recovering from the explosions. Mopsy and Flopsy are comforting each other, sifting through the clothes that Mopsy made. They are all ruined. Benjamin is trying to clean up one part of the burrow, the part where their paw-prints had been recorded throughout their entire bunny lives. Cotton-tail is playing with the ball they used to play with. But it's not the same.

Peter is completely still. He is thinking about what has happened. He looks at his sisters and his cousin. He looks at their home. It is lost. It is all lost. Peter looks across at Bea's cottage, or what is left of it. Bea is rifling through her old paintings, trying to see if any of them have survived. She has never looked so sad.

'This wasn't part of the plan, huh?' asks Cotton-tail, her voice quiet as she looks to her brother for answers. Peter looks at his sister and shakes his head sadly. Peter has never felt more alone.

Chapter Thirteen

PETER'S GRAND PLAN

The streets of London teem with people hurrying to work, while above, a grey sky threatens rain. McGregor is jostled this way and that as he makes his way through the crowd. He is headed back to his flat. The beautiful Windermere countryside is firmly behind him. So is Peter. So is Bea.

As McGregor walks past Harrods, he stops and looks at the new window display. His life in the toy department seems so long ago. He can see his own reflection in the window.

Lost in thoughts of his time there, it takes McGregor a moment to realize someone else's reflection is also in the window. And that someone is standing beside him. It is the General Manager of Harrods. McGregor steps back quickly, his cheeks colouring with embarrassment.

'Thomas! I thought it was you,' she says, smiling. Even after everything that happened, she is pleased to see her past employee. McGregor was mostly always good at his job. 'I've been trying to call you.'

'There's no reception in the country,' says McGregor.

'How barbaric,' says the General Manager. She gives a little twitch at the thought of not being able to use her phone.

'One of its many beauties, actually,' says McGregor.

'I have some good news. Bannerman's no longer with us. We want you back.'

'What happened?' asks McGregor.

'He fist-bumped his uncle in the face. Says it was an accident. Either way, job's open again. Are you interested?'

McGregor turns to his reflection and pauses to think for a moment.

'Am I?' he asks. The General Manager joins him in his reflection once more. Does he want his old job back? Without Bea there's no reason to go back to the countryside. London is where he belongs. He decides to accept the job.

Back at Bea's cottage, or rather, what is left of Bea's cottage, Peter watches Bea packing away the destroyed parts of her home. Her bike is a dented wreck. She tries to give the bell a ring, but it comes out as a muffled, sad sound. Bea kneels down, sighing, and gives Peter a nuzzle.

'Hey, sweetie,' says Bea, 'sorry about your home. This was all my fault. I should've never brought him into our lives.'

Bea picks up a painting she had done of McGregor and frowns at it.

'Such a jerk. Going after you like that. And you not doing anything to goad him. Just minding your own business. A complete innocent.'

Peter looks away, feeling very, very guilty.

'The sad truth is, I actually fell for him. I could have loved him, even. I did love him.' Bea wipes away an angry tear that is falling down her cheek. 'Guess it's back to real life for me. Stop this silly painting and go back home.'

Bea is heartbroken. So is Peter. He looks around, desperate for some way to make it better. She cannot leave! This is not how it was supposed to go. He looks down at the ground. Bea cleans off some dirt and soot from Peter's jacket.

'I do swear it seems like you understand me,' she whispers.

Later that day, Peter makes his way through McGregor's destroyed garden and into the house.

He walks up to the portrait of his parents, which is still where the triplets hung it during the party. It feels like a lifetime ago. So much has changed since then, since the death of Old Mr. McGregor.

'I messed up, guys. Really bad,' says Peter to his mum and dad.

And if this tale was based on a different kind of storybook, Peter's parents would say something like this:

'You have made a mess of things,' says Peter's mother.

'You haven't really been trying to protect Bea, you're just scared of losing her,' says Peter's father.

'But sharing love is not losing love. Love is infinite. You think we loved you any less after we had the girls?' says Peter's mother.

'I thought somehow going into the garden was a connection to you, Dad. Then she came into our lives, and I was scared of losing her, too. I just got confused,' says Peter, shaking his head at himself, at his mistake.

'You've got a good heart, Peter. You just lost your way,' says his father.

'What should I do?' he asks his parents, needing their help more than ever.

'Oh, no. We don't give solutions, we just highlight emotional themes,' says Peter's mother.

For, you see, this tale isn't based on that kind of storybook. Peter is still looking at the portrait, waiting. But there is nothing his parents can say to him. It is just a painting, after all. Deflated, he turns his back on the portrait. Peter walks out of the house, determined, his shoulders back. He knows exactly what he has to do.

Peter returns to what is left of the burrow and gathers his family into a huddle.

'I'm going to London to bring McGregor back,' says Peter.

'Why would you bring back the murderer who's been trying to murder us?' asks Flopsy.

Peter pauses and thinks for a moment, choosing his words carefully.

'Because Bea likes him. And she deserves to be happy,' says Peter. He has figured out how to make Bea happy again. He can fix this mess. He knows he can!

'You mean the only way we can go back to how it was before is by playing love-doctor to two humans?' asks Mopsy.

'It does sound crazy when you say it out loud but I caused all of this and I let you all down. I'm really sorry,' continues Peter. 'I prepared a speech.' Peter reads from the piece of paper. 'I should've listened to you, Benjamin. Not just about this. About everything. You're so much wiser than me. It wasn't about the garden,' Peter says and touches his jacket, his dad's jacket. 'I don't know where I'd be without you.'

'In a pie, probably,' says Benjamin, with a little chuckle. He smiles at Peter. Peter smiles back and then looks again at each of his little sisters. He loves them all so much, he never wants to risk their lives or their happiness ever again. They are all the family he has got.

'When's she leaving?' Cotton-tail breaks the silence.

Peter swaps from caring-brother mode to battle-brother mode.

'Since we don't know train schedules or really where she's going or even how to tell time, I'm just assuming very soon. Can you stall her?' Peter asks his sisters.

The other bunnies all nod, like the soldiers they are. Peter gives them a quick, tight hug, smiles and heads off before quickly turning back.

'Also, I didn't kill old McGregor. He died of a

heart attack,' says Peter with a sheepish grin.

'We know,' says Flopsy.

'Yeah,' says Mopsy.

'The whole time,' says Cotton-tail.

'We thought you needed a victory,' says Benjamin.

'OK then,' says Peter, his eyes brimming with love before he leaves again. This time for real.

Peter makes his way across McGregor's garden. Laser-focus with a half-thought-out plan. This is what a hero looks like. Or a lunatic. The line between the two is very blurred. They just tend not to tell stories about lunatics.

Then, out of nowhere, Benjamin comes running up to Peter.

'Come on. We gotta catch a train,' he says, out of breath.

'You're coming with me?' Peter cannot help the smile that is now on his face. He doesn't have to do this alone!

'Of course. Cousins for life.'

'You got this,' says Peter.

'I got this,' says Benjamin.

Peter nods at his cousin. Between the two of them, Peter knows they can fix everything. He shouts, 'We've got thi–'

He stops mid-sentence and turns awkwardly to Benjamin.

'That was . . . that was supposed to be both of us,' Peter explains. 'You know, doing the "We've got this" thing together?'

'Ohhh, right. Sorry, I messed that up,' says Benjamin.

'No biggie. Let's go again,' says a determined Peter.

'We've got this!' Benjamin blurts out.

Peter sighs. 'Let's go on three. One –'

'Two, three –' counts Benjamin.

'We've got this!' the cousins shout, almost in unison but not quite. Not even heroes can be perfect all the time.

Chapter Fourteen

TWO RABBITS HIT THE TOWN

Peter and Benjamin find themselves in the crush of Windermere train station and just manage to jump on board the London-bound train as it leaves the platform.

'This train goes right to where McGregor works? How does it know?' Benjamin asks, suddenly worried they will end up in the wrong place. That would not be a great way to begin their mission.

'No, it just goes to London,' says Peter.

'We don't know how to get around London,' says Benjamin, working himself up into a panic. 'We thought that town with the square was London. You said London was even bigger than that. What do we do?' he continues as the train rumbles through the countryside.

'Coming through, coming through,' shouts a very familiar voice, belonging to a very familiar mouse.

It's Johnny Town-mouse and he is being followed by Peter and Benjamin. Benjamin's eyes are wide, his mouth open. He is in awe of this mouse who seems to know everything.

'Well, well, well, two country rabbits need help from a town-mouse on how to navigate the big city. Isn't that ironic,' says Johnny Town-mouse.

'No, it's exactly as expected,' says Benjamin.

'You! You're the brains behind this operation, aren't you?' Johnny points at Benjamin before a shoe comes and kicks him way, way into the air. Peter and Benjamin are shocked. They freeze. What has happened to Johnny? He is their only guide to London. They won't be able to complete their mission without him. They need him!

'There's a thing called street smarts. You can't teach it. Follow me. And stay low,' says Johnny Town-mouse as he comes back down without his hat. He is fine. The mission is still on track.

Inside his London flat, McGregor is at the window, playing a tuba. He stops when he spots a bird and picks up his binoculars. He whips out his notebook and records what he has just seen. PIGEON. Above is written another bird sighting. PIGEON. And above that, McGregor has written yet another bird sighting. PIGEON. The page is one long list of pigeon sightings. He is definitely not in the country any more.

There is a knock at the door. Thomas turns on the stereo on the way to answer it and the tuba starts playing again.

'Thomas McGregor? Sign here, please.' It's the postman. 'From the Land Registry in Windermere. Looks like you sold that place you inherited. Congratulations.'

McGregor signs.

'It's official, then. And with the price you fetched, you will be able to install tempered glass shelving in your new store. And seasonal window decorations.'

'Don't know if I've got it in me any more,' says McGregor, looking down at the envelope. 'And I should really stop telling strangers my business.'

'Sorry I didn't report back sooner, but you've been away. I watered your plant,' says the postman, pointing to a potted plant in the hall outside McGregor's front door.

And in the Windermere countryside, Bea has finally finished packing up her cottage. Flopsy and Mopsy are watching from outside, trying to figure out a way to stall Bea until Peter gets back from London. The sisters look at each other and both seem to have the same idea at the same time. They race off to find Mrs. Tiggy-winkle and get the hedgehog to shower them with her spines. This should keep Bea occupied for a while.

Moments later, the two bunnies present themselves to Bea, spines sticking out of their fur.

'Babies!' cries Bea as she bends down to pluck them out. 'What are you going to do without me?'

The bunnies look down at the ground, their ears drooping at their sides. Mrs. Tiggy-winkle looks on sadly.

Back in London, McGregor has returned to his old job at Harrods. He inspects the toy department as a trail of nervous employees follows behind him.

'Well done all round,' says McGregor.

One of the workers staggers back in surprise at the compliment and accidentally knocks over a display.

The employees all hold their breath, waiting for McGregor to explode. But he doesn't. He just stares all around him.

'Was it always so dark in here? There doesn't

seem to be very much natural light,' says McGregor.

'There's no natural light at all, sir. We're inside,' explains one of the employees, Siobhan.

'How can you live like this?' McGregor shakes his head.

Meanwhile, Peter and Benjamin are being shown the sights of London by Johnny Town-mouse. Johnny loves playing tour guide. They jump on to the back of a black cab as it trundles down Oxford Street, and past the theatres of the West End. Then it's down on to the Tube, a quick whizz along, and back up to street level. On a particularly crowded pavement, Peter looks up to see what everyone is staring at.

'Big Ben,' he says.

'Yeah?' replies Benjamin.

'No, Big Ben!' Peter repeats himself.

'Yes, what? I'm right here!'

'Big Ben!' says Peter, getting more than a little frustrated at his clueless cousin.

'Big Ben, Little Peter, Annoying Mouse, what?' Benjamin says, getting more than a little frustrated at his clueless cousin and turns around to see . . . Big Ben.

'Whoa! Much larger than I thought. Much larger.' Benjamin stares at the impressive clock tower until Peter grabs him and they head off again. They are against the clock after all! Peter, Benjamin and Johnny Town-mouse ride through the streets on the backs of rubbish trucks and hop from one building top to the other. They dodge traffic, people and dogs until, finally, they stop outside Harrods.

'Thanks, Johnny. We owe you one,' says Peter as the bunnies cross the street.

'If you ever do decide to throw another blowout, hook a brother up,' Johnny calls out from the curb.

'Don't think there's going to be another!' Peter yells back.

'Holler at me if there is!'

'There won't be one!' insists Peter.

'But hit me if one pops up!' Johnny Town-mouse insists even more.

'Not going to pop up!'

'Just don't forget me when you're making your list!'

'No list will be made!'

'Well, be sure to reach out when –'

Finally, Johnny is silenced when a car comes and sprays a puddle of water all over him. The rabbits escape into the department store.

Chapter Fifteen

THE GREAT ESCAPE

The rabbits scamper through Harrods, making sure they are not seen by any of the shoppers. Finally, they reach the toy department and scan the aisles for any sign of the man they came for. But McGregor is nowhere to be found. Benjamin jumps up on to a doll's house to get a better look. He surveys the entire department, stopping when he comes eye-to-eye with a girl.

'Aaaahh!' cries Benjamin.

'Talking bunny doll!' says the girl, delighted with what she has just found among the rows and rows of toys. She squeezes Benjamin with all her might.

'I am a rabbit,' says Benjamin, speaking in a robot voice. 'I like carrots.'

The small girl giggles and grabs some plastic food from the doll's house. She then shoves it down poor Benjamin's throat.

'Aaahh!' Benjamin gags and sprays the plastic food everywhere, the robot voice gone.

'Aaahh!' cries the little girl.

'Aaaahhh!' cries yet another voice loudly. Only this one belongs to McGregor himself. He has seen everything that has just happened. How can Benjamin be in his department store? The rabbit should be in Windermere! Far, far away from London! All the shoppers stop and stare at the commotion.

'This isn't happening. You're an illusion. Deep breaths,' McGregor says, more to himself than anyone else. Peter and Benjamin take all this in before scurrying over to him.

'Hey, friend,' says Peter, keeping his voice calm.

McGregor swats at the rabbits with his clipboard. This causes even more of a commotion, just as the General Manager walks by.

'We just want to talk!' says Peter.

'Rabbits don't talk!' says McGregor. 'I *knew* you could talk. Wait, are you talking or am I just hallucinating?'

Unseen by McGregor, Peter makes his way to the top shelf of a nearby display case and sticks his head out upside down.

'You tell me,' says Peter.

McGregor sweeps all the stuffed animals off the display case. It is impossible that rabbits can talk. Impossible.

'McGregor?' says the General Manager, her face a mixture of concern and surprise.

'Help me swat these vermin!' says McGregor, trying to see where Peter is hiding.

'Call Security,' says the General Manager with a big sigh. 'He's gone crackers again.'

McGregor sets off on a rampage through the store, lunging at Peter and Benjamin as they run and duck around the toys. Stuffed animals are scattered everywhere. To the security guards watching through the security cameras, it looks like McGregor is chasing after toys. The shoppers continue to stare, mesmerized by the spectacle. This type of thing never usually happens at Harrods.

McGregor picks up a toy golf club and swings it wildly.

'You've ruined my life!' he screams towards the scampering rabbits.

Peter skids across the floor as the club just misses him. He glides through a swinging door marked 'employees only', with Benjamin hurling himself in after him. They find themselves in a silent, dark storage room. The shelves are crammed full of dolls, games and row upon row of stuffed animals. All is quiet for a moment before McGregor explodes into the small room.

'I will end you, rah-bbit!' he says menacingly.

Benjamin quickly bars the door with a toy tractor. This stops the security guards from getting in behind McGregor. The rabbits need time alone with Thomas, to convince him to come back to Windermere. For Bea.

'You've got to come back with us!' says Peter from somewhere in the room. McGregor looks around, trying to see where the voice is coming from. But Peter is well hidden. 'Back to Bea! She's about to leave! Give up painting and go back home!' Peter tries to explain while moving between the stuffed animals.

'No. She can't do that,' says McGregor.

'I know! That's why you have to stop her.'

'Wait. Are you talking?' McGregor asks again, knowing full well humans and rabbits can't talk to each other. They just can't.

'I don't know, am I?' says Peter, being most unhelpful.

McGregor's anger is back. He swings the toy golf club in the direction of the voice.

'She wants nothing to do with me!' Another swing. Another miss.

'That's because she thinks this was all your fault! But we both know I had a little, tiny something to do with it,' says Peter, regret in his voice.

Bea can't leave because of what he has done. She just can't.

' "Little, tiny"?' says McGregor swinging again, missing again.

'Let's not put a percentage on it. Just don't give up on her.'

'But I broke her heart! I deserve no happiness,' says McGregor, shaking his head sadly.

'Yes, you do! You both do!' Peter jumps as the club comes for him again.

'Why am I navigating my feelings with a talking rabbit?!' McGregor can't quite believe how his day is panning out.

'Am I talking?' asks Peter.

Benjamin is trying his best to keep track of the conversation while holding the door closed against the security guards on the other side. Suddenly, Peter scampers down from the shelves and appears in front of McGregor.

Thomas gasps and reaches for a new weapon – two Slinkys. He deftly unsheathes them from their boxes and waves them high. He does not trust Peter Rabbit.

'I just wanted you gone. I didn't think of anyone but myself,' Peter starts to explain. 'I'm sorry I electrocuted you. I'm sorry I put traps on your head. I'm sorry I tried to kill you with blackberries. I'm sorry I rubbed my bottom on your hairbrush. I'm sorry –'

'Wait, what?' asks McGregor, incredulously. Peter's last confession prompts McGregor to interrupt.

'Nothing. Stay focused. You can kill me if you want, but you have to go after Bea. She's much more important than me and you,' says Peter. It's the best he can do. He hopes it's enough.

'How do I know this isn't a trick?' says McGregor, giving Peter a side-eyed glance.

'You don't. You'll just have to trust me.' Peter walks right up to McGregor, unprotected. He's giving himself up to his sworn enemy. If McGregor wants to end it right here, right now, now is the time. 'This is for Bea.'

McGregor releases the Slinkys.

'I like her so much.'

'So do I,' says Peter.

Rabbit and human turn to look at each other. They have found common ground. Then, McGregor gives Peter a slight nod. Peter nods back.

BANG! BANG! BANG!

The door nearly bounces out of its frame.

'McGregor! Unlock this door!' yells a security guard from the other side.

McGregor moves to the edge of the room and

starts manically clearing the top shelf of stuffed rabbits, throwing them on the ground. Peter and Benjamin look at each other. Has McGregor gone crazy again? No. They can now see he is clearing the area near a small window.

Moments later and McGregor manages to get this head, then his torso, then his waist and finally his legs, through the small opening, all with the help of Peter and Benjamin, who follow closely behind. Unfortunately, the small window leads to a ledge, five storeys high. McGregor peers over the side.

'McGregor!'

Thomas and the rabbits turn to see the General Manager and two security guards poking their heads out the window. Peter and Benjamin shove McGregor over the side into a huge bin below. Thankfully, it's filled with cardboard boxes.

The security guards climb out on to the ledge. The rabbits leap to freedom after McGregor. First Peter. Then Benjamin.

McGregor, Peter and Benjamin race through the crowded London streets before jumping on a train and then a bus and then any other form of transport to get them back to the beautiful Windermere countryside.

And so the two former enemies (and Benjamin)

set out across the country, their loved one waiting. Happiness in the balance. It is dangerous, gutsy, exciting and, in a story like this, pretty much a journey guaranteed to succeed.

Chapter Sixteen

TELLING BEA THE TRUTH

Outside Bea's cottage, Betty pulls up with her taxi, ready to take Bea away. Cotton-tail comes up with an idea to stall Bea's plans. She stuffs carrots into the taxi's tail pipe just as Bea gets in. Betty starts up the car and it conks out immediately.

Just then Mrs. Tiggy-winkle scurries up, unseen by Betty or Bea, and backs her quilled behind up to the tyre.

PFFFT! The tyre lets out a sad noise as it deflates. This taxi isn't going anywhere. The animals share smiles with each other.

'This is starting to feel a bit cartoony,' says Bea with a sigh.

Eventually, Betty manages to get the taxi up and running. She pulls the car away from the cottage towards the gate. But the animals are ready for this.

'Now!' yells Pigling Bland.

Tommy Brock gives Felix D'Eer a little shove.

Felix stops just in front of the taxi. He looks into the . . .

'Headlights,' Felix says, in a trance.

'Stupid daytime running lights. Sure they save lives, but they don't help get you around a deer when you're trying to catch a train,' says Betty.

The bunnies gather around the gates. Cotton-tail is on alert. She puts her ear to the ground.

'A man's coming. On a motorcycle . . . with two tiny men holding on?' Cotton-tail hits her ear, trying to fix her signal. Two tiny men? Surely that can't be right.

But sure enough, McGregor, Peter and Benjamin zoom up the road on a motorcycle, the rabbits holding on tight to Thomas.

The taxi is finally free of Felix's trance and is heading out. McGregor slams on the brakes and slides up to the taxi. The sudden stop launches Peter and Benjamin from the bike. Thomas gets off and runs to Bea, who has watched the dramatic arrival and has clambered out of the taxi.

'Don't leave! You once said we all have a place in this world. This is your place. You shouldn't have to leave it because of me.' McGregor chokes a little on the dust kicked up by the motorcycle as his words tumble from his mouth.

'Were they . . . with you?' Bea asks, looking from

McGregor to Peter and Benjamin and back to McGregor. She's trying to get her head around what, exactly, is happening.

'They came to London and talked me into coming back. Well, probably didn't talk, probably all in my head, not the point,' says McGregor, willing himself to focus. 'I love you, Bea. And I'm sorry I did this to you.'

'You tried to kill them. You destroyed their home. You destroyed my home.' Bea crosses her arms.

'I didn't mean for any of that to happen. We just got caught up in our fight,' says McGregor not explaining the situation all that well.

'"Our fight." You still blame them. Pathetic,' says Bea, shaking her head. 'Let's go, Betty.'

McGregor starts towards Bea but Betty steps between them.

'Let's try to save what little dignity we have left,' she suggests.

'It was all my doing. I take full responsibility,' surrenders McGregor.

'My hero. Admitting it was you who blew up their burrow. And not, as you claim, a rabbit pushing a detonator button,' says Bea, unconvinced by McGregor and anything he has to say.

Benjamin, fearing all is lost, jabs Peter. He has to do something. Peter grasps for an idea, anything to help McGregor explain that it was not all his fault. Peter's got it!

He races off towards the destroyed burrow. They all stop talking and watch Peter as he stops, picks something up, and races back again. He goes to Bea and looks up at her.

'Are you OK, sweetie?' says Bea, kneeling down to Peter's level.

Peter looks her in the eye. He's a humbled rabbit but he's determined to help Bea understand. He takes out the remote control from his pocket and pushes it over and over.

Click, click, click.

'What?' says Bea as she begins to understand.

Click, click, click.

'You were part of this?' she continues.

Peter approaches Bea. Then, he puts his forehead to Bea's forehead, apologizing. He's sorry. He's very, very sorry.

'I can't believe it,' says Bea. She looks up at McGregor. He was telling the truth. 'This is a lot to process.'

'We both love you,' says McGregor, his voice soft, his heart on his sleeve. He walks towards Bea, petting Peter without realizing. He's too distracted by just how beautiful she is. 'Forgive us?'

Peter looks into her eyes. So does McGregor.

Bea is at a loss. But before she can answer, a blast of noise breaks the tension in the air. A Range Rover comes tearing up the road at a ridiculous speed. It's driven by the self-entitled city dwellers, Derek and Sarabeth, that McGregor nearly ran over some time ago.

'Mind moving out the way? Our driveway and all,' says Derek, a grimace stuck to his face.

'Perfect country gem. Look at the sunflowers!' says Sarabeth as she holds up the sales papers McGregor signed, along with the brochure of the manor with rows of sunflowers.

'Sorry, it's not for sale,' says McGregor, looking quickly at Bea.

'Yeah, 'cause it's already sold. We bought it,' says the man, looking at McGregor. 'Who are you?'

'The person you bought it from and the person who's cancelling the sale,' says McGregor, standing up a little straighter.

'No. Sale's final. Sorry. This is our new country house,' he says in a determined voice.

Peter can't let this happen. Not after everything they have just gone through. Not after everything is very nearly fixed. He has an idea.

Peter makes a signal with his ears for the rabbits to follow him into the garden.

'And it's perfect. Like a storybook. My stupid

sister's gonna be so jealous,' says Sarabeth, an evil flicker lighting up her face.

'You already sold it?' Bea asks McGregor.

'Yes, but I thought that . . . and . . .' McGregor struggles to find the words that will fix this new mess. He turns back to the couple. 'I hereby declare the sale null and void.' He reaches for the contract but the woman keeps it out of reach.

'Sale's been completed. Sorry,' says Derek, smirking at McGregor.

Meanwhile, the rabbits have all sneaked away to the gate of McGregor's garden. Peter turns to Cotton-tail and gestures for her to go under.

'Really? No way!' says Cotton-tail, giving a little squeal and jumping up and down.

'You're ready,' says Peter, as he gives his sister a nod.

Cotton-tail sneaks under the gate. Peter helps her through as the others all fan out.

'It would really mean a lot if you gave it up,' says Bea, trying to persuade these people in their Range Rover that McGregor's manor is not for them. 'There are other houses in the area.'

'Don't want other houses. Want this one. You and your husband need to be off now,' says Sarabeth, catching her husband's smirk.

'I'm not her husband,' says McGregor, blushing

slightly. 'Although, maybe now's the time . . .'

Thomas drops to one knee, only for Bea to pull him straight back up again.

'No,' she says sternly.

'Just got caught up,' mutters McGregor. 'Understood. Lots of work to do.'

'What is that?' Sarabeth, sitting in the Range Rover, asks suddenly, pointing towards the garden.

The humans all look to where she is pointing. The couple get out of the car to have a better look. It's Cotton-tail in the garden, making it rain with a tomato plant. And then a sunflower disappears. Then another. Then they all disappear.

McGregor's face changes from confusion to understanding as it all clicks into place.

'Oh yes. We have a bit of a vermin problem.'

As if sensing a call to arms, the animals scattered around the countryside drop what they are doing. A party. They can sense a party. And, all at once, the humans watch as the animals descend on the garden. Mrs. Tiggy-winkle waddles through, hoping there will be a chance for her to lose her spines again. The squirrels and Pigling Bland follow closely behind. More and more animals arrive, welcomed into the garden by Flopsy and Mopsy at the gate.

'And small furry land animals as well,' McGregor continues to explain to the city dwellers.

In the garden, corn stalks start disappearing. Then, carrots start flying into the sky. Chaos officially arrives at McGregor's manor.

Felix charges at the double gates and they explode, attaching themselves to either side of his antlers. He shakes one off into the garden, and the other into the pond, splashing the new owners. They jump back in horror.

'And also big ones,' says McGregor, trying to hide his smile. 'They seem to think it's their land, too.'

Bea catches on. 'Not quite the perfect country gem you imagined, huh?'

'Eh, this is just the outside,' says Derek with a shrug. 'We'll put up a fence. Or maybe a pool.'

'The house is what we want. So cute. Like a 3D version of a storybook,' says Sarabeth.

The couple head straight for the house. McGregor and Bea exchange a look. Then they see Peter and Benjamin on the wall heading for the back of the garden. McGregor runs off and meets the rabbits at the back door.

As the couple walk towards the house, all seems quiet and empty. It reminds Thomas of when he first arrived, all those months ago.

'Aw, babe, it's perfect,' says Sarabeth as they enter the house.

'And we got it for a steal, too,' says Derek, his chest puffed out. Just then Pigling Bland drops from the chandelier, right in front of them.

Sarabeth lets out a blood-curdling scream, Derek shrieks and Pigling shrieks right back before clomping off into the house. Along the way, he passes a room with hedgehog tossing and some animals trying to banister- surf. It's even wilder than the first party!

The couple take one look and run down the path. As quickly as they can, the pair jump in their car and peel out of the driveway, a cloud of dust billowing behind them. As a final act, Sarabeth tosses the sale paperwork out of the window. They won't be back.

Chapter Seventeen

A GARDEN IS FOR SHARING

McGregor and Bea watch the couple leave from the front door of the manor. Then, they turn inside to see what is going on.

'What a mess you made,' says McGregor, his loud voice causing everyone to look up. 'What a mess you made,' he says again, a smile spreading across his face. Peter gives him a wink.

'Did you just wink?' asks Bea. 'I didn't know you could do that.'

'There's a lot of things you didn't know he can do,' says McGregor. 'Do you forgive us?'

'You know if you stay here, they're going to have the run of the place,' says Bea.

'Nothing would make me happier,' says McGregor, through gritted teeth. He leans in for a kiss.

'No,' says Bea.

'Not even that?' replies McGregor, clearly disappointed. 'I do have a lot of work to do.'

Peter jumps into Bea's arms and goes to nuzzle Bea. She stops him as well.

'You, too,' says Bea. 'It's not that easy.' But she smiles at Peter anyway. Quick as a flash, Peter jumps from her arms as everyone piles out into the garden.

And just like that, it is their garden again. Peter, Benjamin, the triplets and all the other animals run this way and that, eating everything in their path. Peter is their host once more.

'There you go! Knock that over. That's the stuff. Eat away. No Tommy, that's just dirt. Not a vegetable anywhere near your mouth, but knock yourself out,' Peter says before spotting Mr. Tod. 'Come on, you too, Foxy. No, don't want to? Want to eat me instead? Totally get it – I would too if I were you. Just stand around then and watch. Perfect.'

And so, dear readers, take one last look at our hero because everyone, absolutely everyone, can't help but fall in love with Peter Rabbit.

THE END